Will Gatti has a[illegible] passionate abou[illegible]
stories, which didn't help him much in school as he spent most of his time daydreaming. At university he fell in love with an Irish girl and Ireland, and after marrying the girl he spent time in both France and London – doing various things including playing in a band, working for a publisher and teaching – before finally leaving for the west coast of Ireland with his young family. There, he began his writing career.

Will is now head of English at a school in Surrey, but between marking essays he finds time to write. *Rip Runner* is his eighth novel, and the follow-up to the brilliant *The Geek, the Greek and the Pimpernel*.

Praise for *The Geek, the Greek and the Pimpernel*:

'Witty and captivating' *The Times*

'Fast and funny' *Alternative Kidz*

Children's Book of the Week – *The Times Culture*

RIP RUNNER

THIS IS FOR ANNIE
WHO'S SOMEWHERE –
IN THE NEXT ROOM MAYBE

THE Geek, THE Greek AND THE Pimpernel

ORCHARD BOOKS
338 Euston Road, London NW1 3BH
Orchard Books Australia
Level 17/207 Kent St, Sydney, NSW 2000

A Paperback Original
First published in Great Britain in 2008

A CIP catalogue record for this book is available from the British Library.

ISBN 978 1 84616 368 5

1 3 5 7 9 10 8 6 4 2

Printed in Great Britain by CPI Cox & Wyman, Reading, RG1 8EX

The paper and board used in this paperback are natural recyclable products made from wood grown in sustainable forests. The manufacturing processes conform to the environmental regulations of the country of origin.

Orchard Books is a division of Hachette Children's Books, an Hachette Livre UK company

www.hachettelivre.co.uk

Chapter 1

'Michael!'

'Dad?'

'Michael! They want chip and moussaka! My heart breaks.' My dad has a voice louder than a plane taking off.

'Dad, everybody loves your chips.'

My father is as Greek as the pyramids. Joke. Don't panic. My dad is Greek down to his toenails. So is my mother but she's not so noisy and she can sing a lot better than my dad. They sing all the time, and break plates. The customers love it, the plate-breaking. I tell you, in our town plate-breaking is a big deal.

'Michael! Table two! You are sleeping on your feets! Wake up and serve these dishes speedy quick!'

I'm nervous, that's what it is. I feel like I'm on a high wire and there's no safety net.

'I'm here, Dad. Give it to me.'

My dad has lived here for fifteen years but the English he speaks sounds as if it has come through the tumble dryer. When I tell him it's too complicated, he says, 'Complicated? What is complicated? I am Greeks of course I speak complicated. That is why, Michael, we are the cradle of civilisations, good business peoples, best food, best running mans. Olympics, Michael, we Greeks, think it up just like that.' A snap of the fingers, another terrible song about an island with a beautiful donkey on it, and a pinch of my cheek if I'm not quick enough to get out of the way. That's the way he is.

What I don't ever say to him is, if we're so clever, why are we here in Peasely? Who's heard of Peasely? It's a nowhere town with empty streets and, up on the hill, the world's worst school. A little while back the headmaster was actually arrested. That's how bad our school was, and still is. 'Your school, Michael, is a fine now?' says Dad. 'No, Dad, it's same old, same old.' Same old thugs who should have been marched into the next century. 'Ah, this is life, Michael, always sammy holda.' He wipes his eyes and blows his nose.

Still, you get by if you're smart, and I'm smart. Not a genius, but I can think my way round a few corners. I'm small, too. That helps. Who wants to be tall? Tall gets you noticed and my speciality is not being noticed. Oh, and one more thing: I keep to my rules, mostly. I am Michael Patroclus, Michael to my family, Patroclus to the school and Trokka to my friends...and to my enemies.

But they're not the reason my nerves are bungee jumping – it's the running. I'm fast on my feet and running's become my big thing. A seriously major thing.

I entered the first regional qualifier a couple of weeks back, just to see how I'd do – and I won! Then there was the second round and I did better than expected in that, too. So I've done it. I've qualified for the junior Nationals. Tomorrow!

I don't want to think about what comes after that, but of course I do. This is it: if I win I'll automatically be in the British team for the junior Internationals. Can you imagine! Me, Michael Patroclus, representing the country. My dad will go mental. But listen to this: if I do well in the Internationals I could be selected for the junior Olympics!

Dream on, Patroclus! There's no chance. I'm fast, but not that fast, not yet. Focus.

My target is to do as well as I can tomorrow so

that I can qualify to run in the Internationals. They're going to be held down in Cambridge, and there'll be TV and everything. A whole day event. That'll be enough for me.

'Michael! Turn it up! Turn it up!'

Big TV screen. The place is heaving. Friday night, and where do you go in Peasely? You come here: the Patroclus Family Café, except most people call it 'the Greek'. The café is so busy I don't think my mum and dad even have the time to think about moving somewhere else.

And the truth is, I don't mind so much. Not since the Pimpernel made an appearance. That was something! The Pimpernel turned our school upside down and shook it from top to bottom. And nobody knows who he is, apart from me and two others. You see, there are three of us in the gang, and I'm number three. Not that we hang out together, not at school anyhow – wouldn't want anyone putting two and two together and making three. Wouldn't want that at all. Stay invisible: that's rule number one. Rule number one for Patroclus; rule number one for the Pimpernel gang.

More food, more plates, more diners, more noise. And then there he is up on the screen: Ahmet Farsi! I dump my stack of dirty plates in the kitchen, and, ignoring everyone shouting at me to serve them, I get as close to the TV as I can.

Farsi. Sounds fast, doesn't it? Faster than Patroclus, that's for sure. I keep reading about him in the magazines, how he's the top runner in his school: cross country, sprint, everything. Everyone's saying he's maybe the fastest under-15 in the country. There's an amazing story about him, too: he did a real marathon when he was only seven. Ran over a mountain, the article said, ran to warn his village that there were tanks coming. A mountain, can you imagine? And in a war. He must be really tough. And so he's a bit of a star, a shooting star, and a hero as well. Not bad for fourteen.

Except it's not that easy for him. His school wanted him to run in the Nationals, but there's been a load of stuff in the papers about him not being a proper Brit because half his family is still back in his own country, Afghanistan. So he wasn't given the chance to qualify for the British team even though he's been living here for six months. But what's the fuss – he's living here, like we're living here. Patroclus. Farsi. What's the difference? Our café wouldn't be this full if my mum and dad weren't still Greek. It doesn't really matter, though. He'll compete down in Cambridge but for Afghanistan, not us. Our loss.

I turn up the sound: '...No, no, I just like to run. If I run well then people will know a little about my country too and this is a good thing... Yes, I do have sponsors. Blake's. It is one of your famous companies, yes? It is very good, I think.'

There's a cheer when he says that. Half of Peasely love Blake's because they're a big employer here – top of the range runners. Good stuff. Without the Blake's factory, Peasely would go to sleep for good. Mind you, there's a few that don't love them; those who don't work there, I suppose.

'...Most important thing for me is my family. My sister. My sister is very close. Twin, you know. She is coming here soon. My twin. Yes, that makes me happy...' He nods.

He's different to me. My sister drives me up the wall.

'Michael!' my father booms in my ear. 'You run, why not you run like that boy? Eh, like me one time, very fast.'

'Short legs, Papa.' That's her, my sister. 'Short memory, too. Why don't you wake up, Michael, do some work for a change? I have to get ready to go out.' She slaps plates into my hands and disappears. My sister's life, when she's not telling me what to do, is going out, in capital letters, OUT.

More moussaka, more stuffed vines. More chips.

The door swings open with a *ching* and in walks the Geek. She takes a table by the corner and my mother bustles over and makes a fuss; she loves the Geek and is always getting her to take off her glasses and fluff out her black wiry hair. I got to say she looks different when my mother does that, but she's still the Geek: Minou Yabba, clever as a fox, scared of nothing, my ally. She's number two.

I bring her some fat chips. 'Came to wish you luck, Patroclus,' she says.

'Yeah? Thanks.' I'm half thinking that if I do well tomorrow I could find myself running against Ahmet Farsi in the Internationals.

'Patroclus!'

She doesn't half give me a fright when she snaps at me like that. 'What?'

'You look like a zombie. What's the matter with you?'

'Sorry. Are you coming to the race?'

'I'm filming it.'

'Me?'

'You, Patroclus? Don't be silly. I'm following a story.' I forgot to say, the Geek always calls me Patroclus.

Another shout. Another plate: stuffed tomato. No chips.

I pass by her table. 'What story?'

'Break in up at Blake's.'

'Another one! Equipment stolen?'

'Of course.'

'Runners?'

'Patroclus, what's the matter with you?'

I know, I state the obvious sometimes.

'But do you really think a thief will be dumb enough to wear stolen brand-new Blake runners at the race –' I break off as a pint of Peasely's worst comes through the door. Three of them, never less than three: Jaco and two of his mates. The Bins, so called because they love stuffing kids upside down into the school dustbins. Oh, all official of course, appointed by the school, allowed to wear the special red neck scarf. Prefects is what the school calls them; muggers and thugs is what they are. We hoped they would have all been kicked out when Pent, the old headmaster, went to prison. Not a bit of it. Same old, same old, what did I tell you.

'Well, well, Trokka old son,' Jaco says, his round face all creased up in a smile. His little pig eyes aren't smiling though; they never are. 'How's business? Hallo, Mr Patroclus. How about a plate of greasy chips for me and the lads?'

'No greasy chip in this place, no greasy ever, eh!' My dad glowers at them.

'Oh.' Mock surprise. 'Just thought that's where you was all from, Mr P.' Jaco's mates snigger. Stef on the right, Maggot on the left. Always the same. Stef's the one with long crooked teeth – he looks like a real idiot when he sniggers. Maggot's big – he's Jaco's muscles.

'Sammy holda, Michael,' says my dad under his breath, his eyes never leaving the boys, expecting them to start some trouble right there. 'You tell this boys go outside and I give them some chip.'

I tell them.

'No problem,' says Jaco. 'Just wanted to see you were fit for tomorrow's race.'

That takes me by surprise. First I knew that he was interested in running.

'We're all putting a few bob on it.'

'On me?' The Geek gives me a kick from under the table. She's right; it was a stupid question.

Of course that kills Jaco, really sets him off. He tips his head back and laughs, more like a howl though, tears running down his face, and this sets his mates off. Sound like a pack of dogs. 'No, not on you, Trokka,' he says eventually, drying his pig eyes with his sleeve. 'If I thought you was serious competition, you would probably find yourself in the county hospital. Know what I mean?'

I hand them the chips and they saunter off down the dark street, Jaco giving one of his mates a slap round the head for something he said, and all of them laughing. I go back inside.

'Who's Jaco's favourite for the race?' I ask the Geek.

She pulls a face; running has never been one of her interests.

'Blake would know.'

Percy Blake, he's the son of the owner of the company that makes the world's best runners. They call him 'painful Percy' up at school because he seems such a schmuck – wears the wrong clothes, comes bottom in every test and has a giggle that would make a saint swear. Nobody knows what he's really like though, except for me and the Geek. You see, if I'm number three and the Geek is number two, then Percy's number one. He's the Pimpernel.

But he still cheeses me off sometimes. 'I thought he might have called round. Wish me luck, you know.'

'Probably doing jobs for his dad. Do you think Jaco could be mixed up with the break in?'

'Pinching a pair of Blake runners for this bloke he's supporting?'

'Maybe. Perhaps we'll find out tomorrow.'

Tomorrow. The race – and now Jaco's going to be there.

'Good luck, Patroclus.'

'Thanks.'

She calls out good night to my mum and dad and then leaves.

'Michael, you not going to walk your friend home! What kind of boy are you?'

I pull a face. Me, walk the Geek home? She'd have a fit!

The last customer goes and I start clearing the tables. I can't help it but I can't stop worrying about tomorrow. It's not really this business about Jaco, though I wonder who this runner is that they've got. He's not someone from our school or I would know. My real worry is that I'll do something rubbish, like tripping over on the start line, or oversleeping and missing the bus I need to catch to take me there...

I tell you, my brain's rattling like a supermarket trolley on three wheels.

And I'm wondering about this break in, too. Does it really have anything to do with tomorrow's race?

Not possible. I pick up the last plate and add it to the stack on my tray, and I see some joker has scribbled on the table with a felt pen. Why do people do stupid things like this? It just means more cleaning, more scrubbing. It's tiny, spidery writing. One word: 'plate'. Why would anyone write 'plate' on the table?

And then it clicks. The Geek is right; I can be pretty slow sometimes.

I pick up the plate I've added to the stack and turn it over. There's a small envelope stuck to the bottom.

I pull the envelope free and take out the card: *Good luck, Trokka, and keep your eyes peeled. We might be back in business.*

'Michael, what is this that you have there?'

Him? Not possible! I saw everyone who came in tonight, and our place isn't exactly huge: ten tables at the front, and one long one at the back. But he was here, and not even the Geek saw him, or if she did, she'd kept it to herself. And I thought I was Mr Invisible. How does he do it?

'Good Luck card, Dad.'

'Yes, tomorrow you run like windy, Michael, and then you don't need good luck, just a legs like mine.' He gives me a hug and then Mum gives me a hug and then the two of them hug. I tell you, our family, if they're not breaking plates they're hugging. Except for my sister. She's going through the 'touch me and you die' phase.

I say good night. Then I go to my room and prop the card up on my bookshelf. There's no signature, just that little squiggle of a red flower: a pimpernel, it's called. His sign.

And we're back in business.

Chapter 2

Up. Stretch. Wash. Stretch. Juice. Stretch.

Race day. I need to add a new rule to my list: don't think about the race.

Get dressed: shorts, T-shirt. Runners. Blake's, of course, a bit worn now but still the best.

A quick run, just to clear the head. Down to the canal, over the bridge, back through Peasely's little park, across the main street, then sharp right into our road. And home.

More juice. A scoop of yoghurt. Shower. Dress. Sling my sports bag over my shoulder and then a shout goodbye to the parents, and them shouting down to me, then my sister shouting that we're all insane and why are we waking her up and my parents shouting back at her. This is the Patroclus family in wake-up mode. I'm off.

I'm still nervous. I shouldn't be but I am. Stomach as tight as a drum. One hundred metres and the one thousand metres. I'm better over short distances. It comes from all those years of giving the slip to heavyweights like the Maggot.

I try to stick to my new rule.

I catch the eight o'clock bus to Tornby and sit with my bag perched on my knees, looking out of the window at the flat green fields, wondering if either the Geek or Blake will come to watch my races.

Twenty-three minutes later the bus drops me off at the complex. There's already a buzz of people making their way into the building. I walk straight through to the back where the tracks are.

One, I have to register. Two, change. Three, stop fretting. I feel like my sister's stupid hamster when it goes whizzing round on its wheel. Not that she has it any more. Poor old thing snuffed it last winter. I think it was just doing its hibernating winter sleep thing, but she went and buried it in the yard. Full ceremony. Tried to get Dad to sing but he said he had a cold. She got asked out by a boy the following week and that was it; she became monster sister.

Where do I register?

The day's warming and there are people

everywhere. At least there's no sign of Jaco or any of the Bins.

There are flags and white canvas booths and long banners splashing the names of companies sponsoring the event. But no signs as to where you have to register. Blake's have a banner, and Mackie – I think they make bits for tractors – but there's one name I've never seen before, and it's all over the place. SIRP. It makes me think of cough medicine. SIRP SPRINTERS. Giant yellow lettering. Terrible! Worse slogans, though. How's this for lame? BE SIRPRISED. But no one's puking and there even seem to be a few people hanging around their stall.

I decide to hunt down an official, register and then go and check these SIRP people out. I have twenty minutes before my first race so it's better to be busy. I don't want to hang around on the start line miles before anyone else, like some weedy loser.

And then I spot the Geek and wave like a madman. She's all in black, buzzing through the crowd, her camera up to her eye, moving all the time like a funny machine on random remote control, darting this way and that. She sees me and zooms over. I rather hope that she's going to stay and chat but she just gives me a thumbs up and then she's gone. Filming's her total craze at the moment. She thinks she's going to be big in Hollywood.

At last I spot where I have to sign in. So I do that and then head for the yellow booth to check out this SIRP company. I might even pick up some interesting information for Blake.

'Sign up, why don't you, young sir?' The voice is like a slurp of my dad's olive oil. And who says things like 'young sir'?

'Sign up with SIRP, young sir. Win a week at the SIRP Academy.' The man at the booth pauses and arches a black slug eyebrow at me. 'For sporting hopefuls, young sir. Sporting hopefuls, sign up now!' He leans forwards on his counter and holds out a silver biro which he clicks at me. He has one of those old-fashioned cricket blazers with thick red and white stripes, a tan you buy in a bottle, and a head of shiny black hair, gleaming like it's been boot-polished. His shirt pocket has a row of spare silver biros peeking over the top. He switches on a smile. His teeth are so white they almost make me blink. 'I know you,' he oozes, 'don't I?'

'I don't think so.'

'You're from that school. The one in Peasely.' There is only one in Peasely – Staleways, my school. His thumb clicks his biro furiously and I have this odd thought that perhaps he's signalling to someone. Silly, I know, but he's almost as odd as our ex-headmaster Sir (now convict) Pent, who is hopefully residing in a high-security prison in the middle of Dartmoor. 'Name?' The black slug eyebrow arches even higher.

'Patroclus.'

'Ah, yes. Yes. I see.' He consults a list and ticks my name with a flourish. 'Weird name, of course, for a sporting man, but good. Good. Easy to change a name, don't you think?'

'I don't know. I've never thought about it.'

I want to back away but the truth is he has all these runners on a shelf behind him and they look good, a bit like Blake runners – in fact a lot like Blake runners, except they have a pukey yellow flash on the heel. The break in at the Blake's factory! No, it couldn't be possible. Steal the best runners in the country, in the world probably, stick a new flash on them and then put them on public display like this? That would be too stupid for words, but it's some coincidence...

'Looking at the merchandise, I see. Very wise. Got a good eye, have you? Like to try, maybe before your race? What are you in, young sir?'

'The one hundred.'

'The dasher, eh. Patroclus the dasher. Doesn't quite sound right, does it, but you'd like to sign up for a free week at the SIRP Academy of course, and' – there goes the slug eyebrow again – 'I mean FREE!' He gives a triple click on his biro. 'FANTASTIC, eh?' And he stares at me. Just stares. Eyes black as marbles, unblinking. I don't know where to look. It's so rude to stare. Then for half a second I start to feel dizzy. If I didn't know better I'd think he was trying to hypnotise me. Ridiculous or what?

I give myself a shake and ask to see some shoes.

'Sign up.'

'No, thank you, I just want to see your runners, if that's OK.'

There goes the pen again. *Click. Click. Click.* Agitated? Irritated? Or signalling someone? Oh, come on Patroclus. He's just a sleazy salesman. I do this when I'm nervous, I know I do – I see conspiracies coming out of the pavement.

'No? Are you quite sure?' He smiles as if he can read my mind. 'Why not sign now and I'll throw in a pair of these spectacular Sprinters. What do you say?' And his right eye, which isn't staring at me like the other one, blinks at something or someone off to my right.

'No...thanks.' I take a step back. I have to get

changed and this is just as peculiar and unsettling as being at school.

'On your own, are you?'

I glance at my watch. Only five minutes to the race! I can't believe it. What have I been doing? I've got to move or forget about making it to the Internationals.

'Do you need a sponsor, young sir? SIRP is absolutely looking to sponsor young dashers just like you.'

I start to move away.

'SIRP Sprinters, young sir, Patroclus the dasher. Remember the name. SIRP. You heard it here first...'

I can still hear his voice following me as I hurry through the crowd; it's there all the time, oily and somehow familiar, seeping through the chatter: 'Be first with SIRP, young sir. Be first...'

And where's the Geek now? I want her to check him out. Get him on film.

Then the loudspeakers start squawking and the oily voice is sponged away. 'All contestants for the one hundred metres...to the track, now!'

Oh, help! I sprint. My heart is thudding and I've started to sweat. I'm exactly how I don't want to be before a race. But I make it to the changing rooms in double-quick time. In fifty seconds I'm changed and out of the door; two minutes to reach the start line.

And then someone all too familiar steps into my path.

'Hallo, hallo, Trokka.'

Not now! Please, not now. It's Jaco, of course, with his two mates from the night before, and they're blocking my way. I try to jig sideways past them but they spread out, rat-tooth Stef and the Maggot – my least favourite people in the universe. Behind them is a tall, pale boy. Clearly a runner, stick-thin but wiry. He makes me think of a giant stick insect. He's sort of young-old: thin, scraggy hair, white as snow, pale lashes, pinky-looking eyes and an expressionless face. Well, if he's friends with Jaco and his Bins, the best of luck to him.

'Got to go,' I say. 'So if you don't mind...'

'Unfriendly,' says Jaco.

He should know.

'Very,' says Stef.

'My race,' I say. 'Just about to start.' I keep my face blank, a bit like Stick-boy. It's no good looking bothered when you are face to face with Bins; it only makes them worse.

'Oh, you don't want to be late, old son,' Jaco says, but he makes no attempt to move out of my way. 'I never knew you were a runner, Trokka. Bit of a mystery man, aren't you. Is your funny friend a runner, too?' He means the Geek.

'No.' I wish a huge lead weight would come dropping out of the sky and squash him flat. Things like that happen in cartoons all the time.

'This is our boy,' says Jaco patting the Stick's arm. 'He's going to win the one thousand metres. Are you hoping to run in that, Trokka?'

A split second while I try to figure out what the right answer is. I try: 'Yes.'

'That's unlucky for you, old son...'

Well, maybe it is and maybe it isn't because at that second a black-bearded, blue-uniformed official comes avalanching down on us. 'Michael Patroclus!' he barks.

'Yes, sir.'

And then, to my astonishment, he grabs me by the collar. 'Out of the way, boys!' he barks, and hurtles me past Jaco, giving him no time to do anything but blink and step aside.

I hear a 'Yow!' and I think maybe my elbow caught Stef in the ribs. Can't say I care too much and since I'm being propelled through the crowd like a guided missile, I don't even have time to look back and see what the damage is. My heart's banging somewhere up in my throat.

'Thank you very much!... Mind the gap!... Coming through!... Make way!'

And then suddenly we're there, at the start line, and before I can even stammer out a thank you, he's gone. And there's no time to wonder about who he was because the Geek is frantically beckoning me; and the race official is glowering, glancing at his watch and lifting up his starting pistol. I spot the gap that's my lane and barely have time to get down into the start position and dig my toes into the blocks before the pistol cracks and, this is it, I'm hurling myself forwards!

Chapter 3

My first three steps are more stagger than sprint but somehow I'm not trailing. I see the necks of the sprinters right in front of me. Two of them. I want my legs to pump faster. How do you make that happen when you're already going as fast as you can?

Move!

Concentrate!

The two ahead of me fall back a little. I can hear panting in my ears. The slap and scuff of feet on the track. Try!

I really try, and suddenly I'm right between them.

'Patroclus!'

One voice in the hubbub. The Geek, shouting! Nearly makes me lose my stride.

And my chest is bursting, and I'm reaching, and I'm stretching, and I don't know what I'm doing;

and then somehow I'm over the line.

'Patroclus!'

I stumble and bend down, hooping in air as if I haven't taken a breath during the whole of that sprint. Maybe I didn't.

I'm aware of a familiar pair of small feet in well-worn Blake's. I look up into a camera.

'I think you won, Patroclus,' the Geek says.

I can't speak for a minute.

'Patroclus!' She's so impatient sometimes.

Wow! But then I think, maybe she's kidding me? 'Did I?'

'Yes.'

I can't tell if the Geek's smiling or not because she has that camera in front of her face. She always sounds so matter-of-fact, too. Always. My mother would be crying now; my father would be shouting and roaring and slapping people he doesn't know on the shoulder, which is exactly why I didn't want them to come. 'Sleep in,' I told them. 'It's Saturday morning and it's not a big deal; come to the next one.'

I straighten. And it hits me with a wham and I pogo jump about six feet into the air. 'Wow!'

'It wasn't that far,' she says.

'What! What do you mean? I'm in the Internationals now!'

'I'm only joking, Patroclus. Sometimes I don't think you've got a sense of humour.'

I look around for the bearded official. Funny – now that I come to look properly, none of the men and women running this competition are in uniform at all, they just have armbands. So what was he, some sort of security guard? 'Did you see him?' I ask her.

'Who?'

'The bearded man.' I tell the Geek about my set-to with Jaco.

She gives me a funny look and then puts the camera back to her eye and pans. 'Patroclus. There are about a million bearded men here.' She stops. 'What's Jaco doing here anyway? Bins don't do sport.'

'Don't know. They seem to have someone running for them, like he's their mascot, a long skinny stick...'

'Albino.'

'Yes, he is...'

'Seen him,' she says, satisfied with herself. Then: 'Protection.'

'What?'

'That's what they're doing. The Bins, Patroclus, the Bins; that's what they're doing. It's a job, I bet. Instead of stacking shelves, they're earning money looking out for this Stick-boy. Wonder why he needs protecting... There they are!'

They're the other side of the track. The SIRP man with the boot-polish hair and slug eyebrows is talking to them. Jaco is nodding and then he half turns, sees us and does a mocking silent hand clap. Then he turns back and puts his arm around the Stick's shoulder. I wonder if that Stick-boy knows who he's mixing with, or if maybe he doesn't have a choice.

'Have you heard of this SIRP company?'

She shakes her head. 'You know running isn't my thing, Patroclus.'

'Yes, but I wonder if the Blakes are bothered about them. They seem like serious competition.' I tell her about the runners I spotted on display at the SIRP stall and how the boot-polish man tried to get me to sign up. 'Gave me the creeps.'

'Never talk to strangers, Patroclus.'

'Be serious!'

The Geek sounds surprised. 'I always am.'

Why are my friends so complicated? Percy Blake spends half his life being invisible as far as I can see – which sounds a bit upside down, doesn't it, but he's never where you expect him to be, or if he is there, he's in disguise. And Minou is so independent

I sometimes think she's like a foreign country all on her own, if you see what I mean, like France but with just one person in it. And she's still the ultimate Geek. Well, maybe not as much as when she first came to Peasely. Then her glasses seemed to be three times the size of her face, and these days she doesn't even wear them all the time. She always says the wrong thing to the Bins though, just straight out with something to make them mad. Not like me. Quiet as a mouse, me, keeping my nose clean, keeping to my rules to stay safe – but nothing bothers her. She has a habit of walking straight into trouble and then through to the other side.

Well, that's us, some odd team. Not the sort of middle-school pupils anyone's going to take too seriously. Which is just the point really; we're more serious than anyone could possibly guess. Not all the time of course, but when it counts, when it's going to make a difference. Because that's what we have sworn to do: make a difference. You'll see.

'They'll want you even more after your win,' says the Geek, her camera following boot-polish man as he moves away from Jaco and the three runners.

'If they've got Jaco working for them, I'm not having anything to do with them. Anyway, don't you think Blake might get his dad to sponsor me?'

The Geek gives me that sort of 'Oh yes?' look. 'Looking for favours, Patroclus?'

'Why shouldn't I get a sponsor?'

She smiles. 'Blake told me you'd win something today.'

I'm still keeping an eye out for the bearded official but there's no sign of him anywhere. Strange to be around just for that first race. Maybe he's inside the building. Admin or something. I'll ask later on.

'Is Blake here?'

The Geek shrugs. 'Haven't seen him. How long before the one thousand metres?'

'Ten minutes, I think.'

'Don't get into trouble,' she says and then is off, heading in the direction of the SIRP stall.

I go to a stand where there are drinks for the competitors and help myself to a plastic beaker of water. I find a seat. This next race is going to be different to the sprint, more time to think. I wonder about the Stick. Long legs have to be an advantage. He's not the only one with size on his side, though. I've picked out a couple of boys who are almost as tall as him. They look like they could be fast. Of course you can't tell just by looking, but I'm not feeling too confident. I'm fit enough but I just wish I wasn't quite so small.

There are a number of runners who've got supporters from their schools, all wearing matching sweatshirts, matching tracksuits, and with matching teachers by the look of them, too. No one from Staleways, though, apart from me and the Geek. I spot the Stick again and wonder where he comes from. He's still with Jaco and a couple of other boys wearing yellow running vests with a big 'S' on the front. One of the boys breaks away and trots past me to the drinks counter. As he goes by I see the words emblazoned on the back of his vest: SPONSORED BY SIRP. Of course.

Funny how the combination of Jaco and the SIRP man's oily voice made me think about Pent, our old headmaster. If anyone specialised in being fake and creepy and having bullies around him, it was him.

Time to make a move. This time I keep well clear of Jaco and his gang and make my way to the starting place.

I do my stretches and jog part of the circuit, counting my steps to the first bend. Two and a half laps for this race. Far enough.

When I get back to the start line a few of the others are there, fixing their laces, hunkering down and practising starts. No one is talking to anyone else. I'm just about to check which lane I'm supposed to be in, when I become aware of someone standing close behind me.

'Don't turn round, Trokka,' says a quiet voice in my ear. Blake! What did I tell you, Mr Invisible himself.

'Mind out for the ones in the SIRP vests. I've just figured out something about them. Meeting tonight. Watch your feet. Good luck.'

I wait for a beat of five and then stretch and slowly turn round. No one there – the Pimpernel never hangs about.

The Geek, though, is back filming the SIRP team. They aren't liking it one bit. Jaco gives her an aggressive shove. One of the race officials happens to see and there are angry words. Jaco shrugs and rudely turns away. The Geek carries on filming.

Another squawky announcement: 'Take your places for the one thousand.'

Here goes. If I win, I remind myself, maybe it'll be me against Farsi down in Cambridge. He's a distance runner – the one thousand would be chicken nuggets to him.

Focus.

Focus.

I imagine myself wound up tight, metal and steel, shiny and fast.

Focus.

Chapter 4

There are six of us in this race. We're lined up diagonally. I'm lane four. Stick-boy is right on the outside, so he's staggered a good two paces in front of me. The other SIRP runners are to the left and right of me while the remaining competitors are in lanes one and two. None of us talk or look at each other, except me, I can't help sneaking glances at the others. The runner on the inside is bouncing up and down, letting his arms hang loose. He could be fast, I think. In fact, he looks very fast. Then I tell myself not to be stupid, and that makes me smile because I sound just like the Geek telling me off.

On your marks.

I'm down, knees bent, steady.

The white lines stretch in front of me, glimmering, like a runway, like...

Bang!

And where did I end up?

Flat on my face, that's where. How? I didn't take Blake's advice and watch my feet – not carefully enough, anyway, that's how.

I knew the first twenty or thirty metres would be a bit of a jostle as everyone would try to get into the inside lane before the first bend, and that's just what happened. I had reckoned that my best bet was to go flat out, push myself into the front and then let them chase me, rather than the other way round.

So that's what I tried to do. I didn't pull left for the inside lane, but just went straight, which, funnily enough, was what the SIRP runner on my left seemed to be doing too. I could see Stick-boy because he was a bit in front of me, and, just like I thought he would, he immediately started to slice in – though not quite going fast enough to be properly ahead of the rest of us. It was going to be a mangle unless we slowed down and let him in, which wasn't going to happen; and I remember thinking, that's interesting, he needs time to get up to full speed. I mean, he seemed to be pushing himself – his chin was up and his skinny arms were punching the air – but he wasn't going any faster than me. In fact I reckoned if I could just push a tiny bit more, just a little bit, I could clear the runner on my left and cut in myself when it was over.

How long was all this? Seconds, that's all. The way I'm describing it is just the way I told the Geek and Blake later when it was all over, but at the time I was sucking air and straining every muscle in my legs to go faster. I wasn't thinking. I was just doing, reacting.

And then the bend was right there and Stick-boy was in my space and then suddenly my right foot knocked someone else's foot. There was a yell. Not me. And then as I was falling a body crashed into my legs. I hit the ground hard and something went in my ankle, or it felt like it, and I just lay there, my right cheek on the track, my eyes squeezed tight, trying not to believe what had just happened. Not listening to the foul-mouthed cursing coming from the body behind me.

Half a second. One second. How long? I don't know. When I did open my eyes and lift my head, I could see the racers – four of them – stringing round the bend with Stick-boy long-legging it out in front.

I pulled myself up and gingerly tested my weight on my ankle. Sore. Not broken. Maybe only bruised if I was lucky. The boy who had crashed into me was up. He was wearing a yellow SIRP vest. Old oily-voice, the SIRP rep, had his arm around his shoulder and the two of them were arguing with the referee and gesticulating towards me. I thought maybe they were apologising or trying to get the official to come and help me.

Oh, what? Wake up, Patroclus. Maybe the fall had knocked my brain into reverse because I'm sorry to say I don't usually think the best of people round here, especially if they've come within spitting distance of Jaco and his Bins. So it took me half a second to figure it out, and when I did I was up and limping over to them as quickly as I could.

But I was too slow.

'He elbowed me! Made me lose balance...' said the SIRP runner bluntly. He was looking straight at me as I came towards them. It was a stripped down, bald lie, and he didn't even blink, like it was practised. He was tough-looking, not much bigger than me, but his arms were thick, muscly, like he worked out. He should have had a little sticker on his chest saying 'Get Your Face Out Of My Space', or something equally stupid and hard.

'Absolutely right. I...I saw the whole thing,' the SIRP man was saying. 'Clear breach of rules...'

I was cross and getting crosser. Another moment, and I would have exploded just like my dad does, a Patroclus volcanic eruption, and hurled this lying slippery-jack cheat right over the sports complex. Except I'm one of the smallest people I know (only the Geek is smaller) and I'm not much good at hurling anyone anywhere; and I am not my dad. I squeezed my anger down into a clenched fist. My win in the one hundred metres had already qualified me for the Internationals but if I was accused of cheating, or foul practice, that would be it, I'd be out on my ear... 'That's not right!' I appealed to the official. 'He was behind me!'

'Well,' said the official, shaking his head, 'I have to say I didn't quite see...' He hesitated and turned to boot-polish man. 'Look, I'm sure this young chap was just trying hard. I'm sure he didn't mean to...'

'Oh, he did. He most certainly did.' I swear that man was so oily that if I stuck a pin in him he would have leaked enough oil to cook thirty-two portions of lamb kleftiki.

'No, *he* tripped *me*,' I said firmly. 'That's what happened.'

'Calling me a liar?' The runner took a half step towards me as if he wanted to sort me out right there and then. The SIRP man put a hand on his shoulder to restrain him. The runner shrugged it off and squared up to me. He was so full of rubbish he could well have been one of Jaco's gang. Play acting – I ignored him. If he started a fight he would be the one out on his ear.

The official was looking round for help.

'It most certainly was a foul,' persisted the SIRP man. 'I have at least three more witnesses. I think this boy is a cheat and we want to lodge a complaint. Official. And we want to make sure he doesn't run again. Can't have this sort of thing taking place in these races—'

'No, of course—'

The SIRP man ignored the interruption. 'I am sure that you wouldn't want a major company like mine to be contacting the press about bias, would you?'

Three witnesses. I bet: Jaco and his two mates. 'I was in front,' I repeated. 'How could I trip someone behind me? Someone must have seen what really happened.'

'Yes, exactly. I told you. We did.' He smiled.

'I mean someone who doesn't work for your company,' I said.

That wiped away his smile. He blinked slowly as if surprised that I was able to talk back to him. There was a flash of anger there too, behind the oil and the greasy cheating. But before he could say anything else, the Geek appeared at my elbow. 'I have it all on film,' she said simply. 'Do you want to see it?'

The official breathed a sigh of relief. 'Oh, thank goodness. Of course, we can look at it in the office. That's splendid. Now...'

'You'll regret this,' snapped the SIRP man. He pointed a finger at the official. 'I shall take this up at a higher level. I have never seen such obvious bias in my life. As for you,' he looked at me, 'we know your name, Patroclus. On my list, remember. You're finished.'

'That's quite enough, we can sort this out,' said the official, but the SIRP man, with his hand clamped on his runner's shoulder, was already walking away into the crowd. The crisis was over.

'Oh well, storm in a teacup,' said the official. I felt rather sorry for him. He was a decent, red-cheeked man, probably didn't even work full-time for the sports centre, just keen on running and helping out. 'Perhaps we won't bother with the film now. Nothing lost then.'

Except the race.

But I didn't say it. I took my cue from the Geek who nodded and said, 'It's up to you.'

'Then let's leave it. Spoils the day, doesn't it. People accusing other people.'

And that was that.

'Did you really film it?' I asked the Geek.

'Of course. It was a setup. They wanted you out of the action, Patroclus. You should be pleased. They obviously think you're really good.'

'Except I fell.'

'But you won't next time.'

No, that was one thing I promised myself. I wouldn't fall for that again. And I was going to do some serious research on this SIRP company. Like the Pimpernel, I was beginning to put two and two together. I just couldn't believe the 'four' I was coming up with.

The Geek wanted to go back into Peasely but I wanted to watch a couple more races and then go over to the Blake stall and see their new line of running shoes. So we agreed to meet up later to go to Blake's house. 'Big mystery,' she said. 'You know him, up to his eyeballs in something, but wouldn't say, not until the meeting proper.' And then, with a wave, she was off, running for the bus.

I turned back and spent about an hour watching the next two races. Keeping an eye out for any more action from the SIRP runners, particularly the Stick. But I also made sure I didn't run into Jaco.

I went over to the Blake stall, half hoping that Blake might be there, but he wasn't. It didn't matter,

I thought, I reckoned I could ask him that evening if there was any chance of a bit of sponsorship. I mean, why not... And then I caught the bus back to Peasely.

The next bad thing that happened to me that day was as I was walking home from the bus stop.

Chapter 5

'What do you mean, you won? You got no shoes! How you run with no shoes?'

'I won the hundred metres.'

'He won the hundred metres!' My father's eyebrows are so wild and black and gunpowdery, I think maybe they're going to explode.

'I won that race but I lost the one thousand.'

'You lost your shoes!'

'Yes.'

'How you lose your shoes, Michael? We Greeks run over mountains with no shoes. Olympic is Greek. We invent running but why you run with no shoes?' He is not making huge sense but I know what he means. In fact he's not really talking about my bare feet at all; it's my eye that has him all jumbled up and furious. I haven't seen it yet but it burns like a hot pan, and I can't see out of it; my feet are sore too but that's just because I've had to walk back from the park barefoot. I wouldn't have been a match for all those ancient Greek barefoot runners he's going on about. Half a mile on gravel and pavement and they're stinging – though nothing compared to my eye. I just want to go up to my room. I feel so low I could crawl through a crack under the door.

'How you lose your shoes! Anna, look he has no shoe. His feet...how he going to run, this boy!'

My mother has come out of the kitchen and is standing just behind him. She pushes her hair back but for the moment says nothing. It's hard to say anything when my father is simmering like this. The veins on the side of his temple are swollen and throbbing. 'You lose your shoe? You have a fight? You kill someone? Michael, you tell us what you do before, before your mother she have heart attack!'

'Dad, if you just let me explain...'

He throws his hands up in the air and is about to erupt again when my mother takes his arm. 'Shh,' she says and pats him. He opens his mouth. I wait. The battle drums throbbing inside his head; the tribes of Patroclus warriors streaming down from their mountain stronghold on the wild island of Spiros ready to battle with monsters and giants and shadows, hesitate, pause, and then slowly fade. His mouth closes.

'What happen, Michael? Sit.' She makes me sit down, tilts my head to look at my eye, and then lifts my right foot and checks it for cuts. 'Papa,' she says, 'bowl. Hot water. Towel.'

'OK. OK. This is what I am doing.' And he is off, rumbling but happy to be told what to do.

As she cleans my face and bathes my feet, I tell them what happened. Well, I tell them a bit of what happened. I skip the bit about being tripped up in my second race and instead tell them what I can about the incident in the park, without dressing it up, like my father would.

'I didn't see who it was, not properly. There was just the sound of someone, maybe more than one person...' I try to remember exactly what I heard but it was just the sound of running feet on the path behind me. I didn't think much of it; you get people jogging most afternoons around the park. Except I remember thinking, this is the sound of running fast, not jogging. And then someone slammed into my left shoulder, sending me spinning round and I just caught a glimpse of a pale face before my eye connected with a fist and that was it; I was splashed out on the ground for the second time in one day.

I felt my Blake runners being pulled off me but when I tried to haul myself round someone put their foot in the middle of my back and pressed me down, hard. I couldn't move anything except my head, but one eye was closed up and the other was watering with sympathy. No one said anything. Just a grunt, which might have been me, and then the sound of running feet again. Seconds.

I lifted myself up but there was no sight of him or them – must have been them – one to step on me and the other to take the runners. Why would anyone take my runners? My Blake's. They weren't even new. But it did happen, happened at my school in the bad old days, kids getting mugged, mostly by the Bins, the prefects. And the bad old days weren't so long ago. Six months, to be precise, when the old headmaster got arrested.

'And they just took your shoe, your running shoe.' My father shakes his head. I can see this is a personal insult to him; he would have been happier if I had recounted a bloody battle, me against thousands, back to a tree; not much honour in a mugging over a worn pair of shoes. 'This place is... I find this person... This person, it is not those boys who come in here, no?'

My father has threatened to wring Jaco's neck so

many times, I am half worried he might actually do it one day. In the meantime, though, he wrings the tea towel until it twists into a loop.

I shrug. 'Never seen Jaco run anywhere.' Could have been them though. Punishment for winning the one hundred. A little lesson. And they would've been raging that their grubby attempt to have me dumped for cheating just blew up in their faces. No, they didn't like that at all. Well, too bad.

'If I catch this boys, I take his nose and I twist them so,' and he tries to twist the tea towel into another turn but it's already so tight he can't. My mother tells him to check the evening's dishes, so, still squeezing and muttering, 'Sammy holda, this place, sammy holda,' to himself, he stalks into the kitchen.

Then, after putting a cool compress on my eye and bandaging it up so I look like a veteran from the battlefield, my mother sends me up to my room, promising that she and my father can manage the café that night without my help. Clara can help, she says. My sister won't like that but then she doesn't like anything interfering with her social life.

'It's Saturday,' I remind Mum.

'Clara will help,' she says firmly. My mother is the

real boss in the house; Clara and my father are the noisy ones. They storm and shout, mainly at each other, but at me, too – at least Clara does. But if my mother decides on something, that's it. They do what she tells them. So do I. Mostly.

I go up to my room, but I don't lie down. Five o'clock. I switch on my PC and the little TV I have perched on the chest of drawers.

The computer pings, telling me that Instant Messenger has logged a new message. I click to see who it is: no name, but I know the email address.

My place for the meeting. The car will be on the corner of your street at 6.

I type back 'OK'. Then I ping the Geek to see if she still wants to meet me at the corner. One hour. Plenty of time for a bath. Behind me the TV news barks on: immigration problems. Some scandal with one of the camps they have for the unlucky ones who want to come here but who the government doesn't want. Another small fire in the channel tunnel, nobody hurt. Sports news. Farsi's name is mentioned but I don't catch what is said. I go into the bathroom and I'm just about to get into the tub when a familiar voice stops me in my tracks.

'...No, it's really a question of unfair business practices...'

A voice as slick as cat's fur.

'...questionable of course...serious allegations because of our suspicions...yes, under investigation...'

A voice that makes my skin crawl.

'...Blake's, the sports-shoe manufacturer, of course I can't say more... A sorry business, though, when such a reputable firm begins to fall rather low. You see what I mean...'

I ignore Clara who's now standing in the doorway scowling at me – she always wants to be in the bathroom when I am – and tear back into my room.

'Thank you, Minister,' the reporter is saying and there, his pale, phoney, smiling face filling the screen, is Sir Maximus Pent. My ex-headmaster. This is the man who should be inside a maximum-security prison, a prison with mile-high walls tipped with spikes! This is the liar, the cheat, the kidnapper, the fraud. And he's now a minister in the government! Sir Pent, Minister for Sport. I close my good eye and look again. How could anyone let this happen? How could he have wriggled his way out of prison, got himself elected, and coiled his way into government!

I feel tight in my stomach. There's a pulse throbbing under my right eye.

It's so creepy it makes me feel sick.

Angry.

Get a grip, Patroclus!

Am I mistaken? Maybe the bang I got muddled me up. Maybe I'm mistaken...

I check the news on my PC but whatever that last item was about it hasn't filtered onto the internet yet. There's nothing for it but to wait till I can talk to the others, so I pad back to the bathroom to soak away some of the day's badness, and comfort myself by thinking about winning the first race. That was good. One good thing...

But I still can't help thinking about him, Sir Pent, and that creepy man from SIRP... As I lie there, half dozing in the warm water, the two names sort of slide into each other...

Chapter 6

The bath was good but I'm still edgy.

No word back from the Geek and she's usually hovering over her computer when she's at home, stinging off messages like a mad mosquito.

I'm at the corner too early. I can't help it; I'm always early and then I have to stand and wait. It's Saturday night and even our street has a few people strolling along, some heading for our place or for a walk along the canal, a pint in the Anchor. I keep wondering if any of them are looking at me.

Spies.

That mugging came right out of nothing. The park seemed empty and then *wham!*

My eye is sore; it's started to swell.

But who'd want to spy on me?

And why take my shoes?

And has it anything to do with the break in at Blake's?

A gang of kids from school, the year below me, come running up the pavement. 'Hey, Trokka, want a game of footie?' They jostle about me. 'Heard you won a race!'

'Nice one.'

'Wanna play?'

'No. Can't, sorry.'

'Waiting for your girlfriend?' More shoving and jostling. Grinning. There's always one with more mouth than manners.

'No.' I shrug.

Then they're off. Running. The mouthy one trying out a singsong: '*Trokka's got a girlfriend!*' but no one picks it up and his voice gets lost in the general noise they're all making. I'm forgotten. No fun to bait. Don't show what you're really feeling. I learned that rule a long time ago.

They didn't bother me anyway, except that even a bunch of kids milling around draws attention. It's older ones I'm nervous about. The ones who are bored, cruising around Peasely, grubbing sharks looking for something to do. Someone.

Jaco.

Was it one of the Bins who duffed me in the park?

Maybe, but they don't usually care if anyone sees them or not.

Two minutes to six. Why isn't the Geek here? Maybe she went straight out to Blake's. She must have been in a hurry not to leave me a message.

There's an empty shop just up on the corner – used to be an outfitters – you know, clothes, the sort that no one in their right mind would ever wear. Closed down, like half the town. The entrance is set back a little, so I take up position, tucked into the shadow, and when the Blake saloon slowly passes by I duck out and slip onto the back seat without the car even coming to a stop.

I'm on my own, on this mile-wide leather seat and the driver is Blake's dotty dad. I glance back over my shoulder, just to check but there's no one watching, no one I recognise anyhow. A couple of teenagers, talking to someone on a motor scooter, an elderly couple coming out of the café. I turn back.

'Hello, Mr Blake, how are you?' I wonder if he's heard the news about Sir Pent.

'Michael, marvellous, absolutely. Just popped out for something but you know I forgot what it was and there you are popping into the car. Marvellous. Here we go...' And the powerful car surges forwards down the main street, out past the park and into the country. Mr Blake turns up the radio and hums to himself.

What a strange family. I mean, my family is strange, maybe all families are, but the Blakes... Was he serious that he had forgotten why he was driving into Peasely? I don't think so for a moment. I catch his eyes in the mirror, and for a second I see a different person – thoughtful, studying me – and then he's just a cheery absent-minded old buffer again. He seems much older than my father.

Blake's house isn't that far out of town and it isn't that grand either, though it has electric gates which always seem a bit spooky to me. It's like there's some invisible hand opening them – a bit Dracula's castle, if you know what I mean. Not that the Blake house is actually like that at all; it's light and cheery. Mrs Blake is French and spends all her time in the garden. She smiles but doesn't say much, not in English anyway. Blake told us that it was a family tradition that the Blake men always married a Frenchwoman. The Geek, I remember, was quite interested by that. She wanted to know why, but Blake just shrugged and said, 'Why anything?'

Mrs Blake opens the door.

'Hello, Mrs Blake.'

'Michel,' she says. Mrs Blake's been living here for

years but she's still as French as the Eiffel Tower and has a strong accent, stuffed with 'z's. 'How nice you are coming here. Zey are in the back.' She pushes a wisp of hair away from her eyes, smiles vaguely and wanders out into the garden.

I hurry through the big sitting room and the ultra-modern kitchen and into the back where Blake has a den; a kind of workshop-cum-study. It's stuffed with drawings and spidery designs, mainly for running shoes, but there's also a load of new stuff I haven't seen before. There are so many pictures of surfboards and surfers creaming in on giant blue waves, I feel like the wall is about to wash me away. It's his new thing, obviously. Blake gets these sudden passions when he just has to find out everything about something. About four weeks ago it was plumbing. Don't ask me why. It doesn't take Sherlock Holmes to figure out it's surfing now.

Blake and the Geek are sitting at the table, backs to me, heads bowed together, talking so seriously that they don't notice me coming. They must have heard the news about Pent.

'You've bleached your hair!' I exclaim. He has, too. 'You look weird, Blake.' And I'm thinking that now the only place the mysterious Pimpernel can blend into his surroundings is probably in his own kitchen, somewhere between the giant fridge freezer and the giant white cooker.

'Trokka!' Blake swings round, smiling. 'You're here! Excellent!' He's got an open face, as easy to read as the sky – that's what you'd think, anyway. In fact you can't tell at all; his expression is just another mask. He puts them on and off like a pair of shoes.

'He thinks he's one of them,' says the Geek, nodding at one of the pictures of a surfer with bleached hair, shoulders about a mile wide and baggy shorts.

I sometimes think he's actually about half a dozen people and wonder how he doesn't get muddled up.

'See!' Blake stands up so I can see his surfer shorts and surfer T-shirt.

There's not too much surf in Peasely but I don't point this out or the Geek will jump down my throat for being obvious.

'You heard the news about Pent?' I ask.

He's instantly serious again. 'Yes. Sit. Join the war council, Trokka. We've got a bad beach break.'

The Geek ignores the surf speak. Me too. With luck it'll disappear in a couple of days. She frowns. 'Are you all right? What happened to your eye?'

I tell them about my mugging. The Geek mutters something crossly to herself and scribbles slashy black lines on the pad in front of her. Blake glances at her. 'You see!' he says. She nods in agreement and then to me he says, 'I'm sorry, Trokka. I wondered whether to come back with you from Tornby. I thought it could be getting gnarly after the race...'

'Blake,' I say, 'where did you get to? I was looking for you!'

'Oh?' He grins. 'How did you manage to dodge Jaco and the Bins, then...? "Out of the way, boys!" ' he barks suddenly and it's the voice of the black-bearded official back at the race. 'Pimpernel's everywhere, Trokka, you should know that.'

I shake my head. 'People see what they expect to see.' That's what he always tells us: 'Disguise isn't hiding yourself; it's being obvious.' He makes it sound easy but I don't think it is at all – unless you're a Blake, maybe. They've all been the Pimpernel at one time or another, perhaps even before the famous one who played cat and mouse with the French guillotine back in the 1790s.

'Wicked win by the way, Trokka. Rooting for you all the time, of course, but I never knew you could sprint quite as fast as that. Dad was impressed.'

'I've been practising. Why did you think there might be trouble?'

He frowns. 'Because I think there's a war on. And

so does my father. He's got so worried he hardly makes sense any more. Not when it comes to business. Now there's this new company, SIRP, breathing down our necks, and Pent is out and bad-mouthing Blake's. You know, serious bad publicity and...'

This is all tumbling out too fast. 'Hang on! War? What war? Who's invaded who?' Blake sometimes talks in poster-sized capital letters, making a big deal out of nothing.

'Minou agrees, too. Don't you, Minou? All the signs are there, right there, and I just think although we're the target at the moment...'

'We? In half a second I expect you're going to tell me why I got mugged.'

'Your runners,' says Minou flatly.

'What! How could you know that!'

My expression must have been something because the Geek smiles and she doesn't do that too often. Blake twists round the sheet of paper they'd both been looking at when I came in. It turns out to be a UK map with half a dozen black crosses marked on it. 'Blake runners,' he says. 'Can't get them for love or money at the moment, and you know why not? Because here, here, here,' his finger jabs at all the crosses, 'are the factories and retail outlets that have either been ransacked or firebombed, or maybe both, in the last thirty-six hours. Blake stocks are almost down to zero. The old family business is getting mashed; we're heading for a wipeout. That's just what I was telling Minou when you came in. It's war, Trokka.'

'So you mean a business war, right? Competition. Not more than that?'

Minou makes a face but says nothing.

They're both looking at me, waiting. There's something I should know, something I should have figured out. I can feel the locks and wheels spin and click in my brain. Of course. I've been as blind as Jaco and his mates, not seeing what was right under my nose. SIRP. Sir Pent. I knew it already. I knew it as I was lolling in the bath. I just hadn't put the two together. It's as clear as day now.

'SIRP.' I say it out loud. 'Sir P. Sirp. SIRP.'

'You've got it in one, Trokka.'

'How's he do it? Out of prison and straight into government? I heard him on the TV earlier.'

'Always had friends in high places.'

'Or low,' adds Minou. 'Deep down.'

Blake and I both look at her blankly.

She shrugs. 'Devil always looks after his own. That's what my mum says.'

'Why does she say that?'

'Cos it's what they say in her church the whole time. See the devil round every corner. Maybe they're right.'

Maybe they are.

SIRP.

Sir P.

Sir Pent.

Serpent. That's what I always used to call him when I thought about him at all. Sir Pent. Poison. What kind of a government would elect someone like him anyway, someone with a criminal record? Perhaps the Geek is right. A velvet-tongued devil in a velvet suit? No, that's stupid. But it makes me think of something else. 'Is this the first time your family have come up against him?' I ask Blake.

'Why?'

'Just wondered whether his family goes back, like yours. Old scores to settle.'

'Family feud?'

'Yes.' My family knows all about those sort of things. 'Greeks,' my father says, 'we make our friends for life; but our enemies we make for ever.'

'Don't know. Maybe. My dad's never said but I suppose the family's always been up against people like him. The bottom line is that our business – Pimpernel business – is to deal with him, because I think knocking out Blake's is just step one in whatever nasty scheme he's hatching. Agreed?' He gives us the 'this is serious' expression. He still looks weird with the bleached hair, though.

'Agreed,' we both say.

I register that the Geek is studying my face. 'You need a nanny, Patroclus.'

'No, but eyes in the back of my head might help. Mightn't get tripped or mugged so easily.'

Blake nods. 'That's a seriously good idea, Trokka. You could see a peeling wave without having to turn your head—'

'Blake!' The Geek cuts him short.

'OK, all right, just thinking out loud. I know, a plan is what we need.'

The three of us fall silent, all looking at the map with the black crosses on it.

'Sir Pent has only just made himself known,' says Blake after a moment. 'No mention of his imprisonment. None of his release. Nothing in the press about his appointment as minister. Don't you think that's strange? Like there was no yesterday.'

'A bit like Groundhog Day,' says the Geek. 'I loved that film.'

But I'm not listening. My mind is at last beginning

to click into action. 'The robberies, they're not just to hit your business, are they? Isn't it like he's looking for something?'

The Geek nods. 'That's what I said.'

'The secret of Blake's special runners,' says Blake. 'Yes. I suspect you're right about that being part of it.'

'And I got mugged because I won a race today and someone from SIRP reckoned that maybe it was down to some clever bit of technical gadgetry in the soles of my feet.'

'Soles of your runners,' corrects the Geek.

I look at Blake. 'Was there?'

'Was there what?'

'Some trickery in my runners. You gave them to me. You should know.'

'Trickery, Trokka! Of course not. You won your race because you ran faster than anyone else and you used your head, too. That's the secret. Blake runners can give you an edge, that's all.'

That's for sure. I've seen him and the Geek climbing straight up the outside of the school, like a pair of spiders, shoes sticking to the wall like magnets.

'But it's true that we're working on a new line, something that would give the person running a bigger first stride. Our technicians have put together a couple of prototypes.'

'And that's what they're doing, isn't it?' I say. 'Trying to find the design centre? They know you've these prototypes you're talking about and they want them. They're not just burning you out, they're cutting up and analysing every runner you've ever made. Boffins and white coats, Blake, that's what they're looking for. Have they found it, the Blake design centre?'

'Where are your boffins?' asks the Geek.

'Where are your white coats?' I ask.

Blake pulls a face. Meet goofy Blake – the Blake who goes to our school, except then he wears fat glasses and his ears seem to stick out more.

'Well?'

'Well, it's a bit embarrassing really.'

'Why?'

'We're the design centre.'

'Who's we?'

'Me and Dad, my father. It's just us, tinkering, getting ideas...'

'And you work out the stuff?'

'Stuff?' He looks blank.

'Patroclus means the technology, the science,' says the Geek crisply. Her expression suggests she finds it hard to believe that Blake has much of a clue about science.

'Oh, yes. It's not that difficult...'

And I find that hard to believe; I remember the trick running shoes that, at the press of a control button, went so sticky that whoever was wearing them got stuck instantly to the spot. Not rocket science maybe, but clever.

'And for anything that stumps us, we just call up a friend or two. You see, no razor-wire fences or patrolling guards, just us, me and Dad.' He does the high-pitch nerd giggle he usually reserves for school. It really puts your teeth on edge. I always think it sounds bad enough to turn a chicken into a psycho-killer, but at school it makes everyone back away. They think he's mad.

'No one's tried to break in here?' asks the Geek.

The giggle is switched off. 'No.'

'But they will?'

'Yes.'

I'm not sure who says it first but we all have an idea – pretty much the same one, too.

'The next race, the International, is the key. If Pent has a first-class runner...'

'And his runner wins it...'

'If he does, he's set up. His runner will be in the junior Olympics...'

'And if he wins again...'

'...Everyone will want SIRP Sprinters. He'll have it wrapped up. Pent will have a global empire.'

'A finger in every pie.'

'A foot in every door.'

'In every country.'

Like some world serpent, I think, coiling around everything. 'We have to beat him.'

'At the first hurdle. Exactly.'

'Now what he needs is: one, a really fast runner, and two, the formula to the newest, absolutely most top-secret Blake design.'

'He has a runner,' I say. 'Stick-boy. Very fast, and a team to back him. Who do we have?'

'You,' says the Geek.

'Don't be crazy.'

Blake looks at me. 'Actually, you will run, Trokka, and that's a fact.'

'I got through the Nationals, Blake, and that was only for the one hundred metres. I'll be wiped, zeroed in the Internationals. As for making it into the Olympic team...'

'You'll make it.' He puts up his hand to stop more protests. 'We need you. That is, the Pimpernel needs you. You want to stop Pent, don't you?'

'Of course.'

'And you wouldn't mind being sponsored by Blake's?'

'Are you kidding! It's just...'

'Don't worry, Trokka, it won't all be down to you. I think I can safely say that I have someone who can beat Stick-boy, but since anyone sponsored by SIRP is bound to cheat and they showed us exactly how they operate in today's race, we need to be ready.'

I breathe a sigh of relief. 'I'm the backup.'

'Yes. And the second thing Pent and his team need is a pair of top-of-the range, high-performance Blake runners. I think we can provide them with that. What do you say?'

'A Trojan horse, you mean.' Something that looks good but will bring disaster. I like this.

'Beware Greeks bearing gifts,' he says.

And we both smile. On the same wavelength.

The Geek is cross. 'What has this got to do with either Greeks or horses? I don't understand.'

'They're going to break in here and find what they expect to find.'

'Except the runners will have some very special features to ensure that whoever is using them will lose.'

'Will they fall for it?'

'Of course. They'll copy the design even if they

don't understand what all the elements signify. I already have a couple of ideas,' Blake says, beginning to scribble curvy shapes and squiggly numbers on the edge of the map.

'That just leaves this someone who can beat the Stick,' I say. 'Who do you have in mind?'

And then the front door bell rings.

Chapter 7

'Hello...Percy?'

I can't believe it!

It's Farsi, the young champion from Afghanistan, taller than he looked on TV and with a soft, hesitant voice. He's looking at Blake as if he's not quite sure it's him. Probably hasn't seen him with his snow-top head.

'Blake! You might have told us who was coming round! I mean, why didn't you say something?'

He flaps his hand, shutting me up. 'Ahmet!' he says. 'Come in! Meet my clubbies!'

The Geek and I swap looks. Clubbies? What are clubbies? His surf-speak, I suppose. He's changed again, just that tiny change that makes him more Percy, less Blake the Pimpernel.

'Blake's are sponsoring him,' he says to the Geek.

'Didn't I tell you? Sand for brains, that's me!' He gives the giggle. Ahmet takes a step back to the door, startled. Blake ploughs on. 'We reckon he's going to be able to finish his schooling here and his twin can join him. Same school. That's the plan, Ahmet, isn't it?'

'I hope, but there is much problem.'

Blake sweeps away the problem, whatever it is, with a wave of his hand. 'It's a blow out you couldn't run in our Nationals but you've got Cambridge, running for your own country. Then it's the big beach break – the J.O. is his thing,' Blake says to the Geek and me and rubs his hands. 'You're looking for gold, Ahmet.'

J.O. The junior Olympics. I'd give anything to make the grade for a chance to run in that.

'Shake hands with the Trokka – he's my Greek clubbie.'

'You are Michael?' Ahmet says to me. I think I have a stupid grin stuck on my face.

The Geek nudges me to say something.

Rule ten: don't grovel and weasel and generally suck up to people you admire. Grinning isn't sucking up. 'Yes. Hello.'

'You are runner, yes? Percy tells me that he has good friend who runs fast. And I think, forgive me,' he says, turning to the Geek, 'you do not run, no?'

'No,' she says, and then, I can hardly believe it, the Geek just sits him down and starts to chat like she's known him half her life, while Mrs Blake sweeps in bringing little pastries and drinks. Ahmet is more polite than anyone I've ever met, thanking Mrs Blake for her kindness and hospitality and offering her his seat. Mrs Blake smiles and then makes a little 'Oh!' noise and disappears into the garden, reappearing minutes later with a tiny, blood-red rose which she lays on the table in front of Farsi. He picks it up and breathes in the scent.

'In our garden in Kabul,' he says quietly, 'before the bombs, we had such a rose.'

'Of course, of course, and always so beautiful,' she says. I think she wants to pat him on the cheek but I see Blake discreetly signalling her, and she smiles and goes out of the room, leaving the four of us alone.

He's neat and solemn: pressed blue jeans, polished black shoes. I don't remember when I last wore black shoes. As for cleaning them, with polish? Never. He's wearing a skinny blue cotton jacket zipped up to the collar and buttoned at the cuffs. My mum would love him so much she would probably fold him up and tuck him into a drawer. It's weird sitting right opposite someone who you've seen on widescreen TV. His face is thin, sort of pointy. He makes me think of a bird, a hawk maybe, but they've got mad eyes; there's nothing mad about him – just serious. Serious, and, I suddenly realise, worried.

'Your sister,' says the Geek. 'You said there's a problem.'

'That's right,' says Blake. 'We expected the two of you tonight. You said her flight was due this afternoon. What happened?'

'They do not let her into the country.'

'What!' Blake is up on his feet. 'We had it all sorted! Did you tell my father? What did Immigration say?'

'I did not say to your father. He seem to have much on his mind. Immigration?' He pulls a face. 'They say much that I do not understand: numbers, papers... I see her come off the plane. And then I waited, one hour, two hour, for her to come through. No one says anything to me. No one. And when I find a man, official, officer. He just ask for my paper, my passport. He looks like he wants to put me on a plane out of the country. I tell him I am athlete, a competitor. He says, "Oh yes, you do a lot of running in your country do you, up and down mountains, like a goat."'

He is controlled when he is telling us all this, but I can see the anger, icy-sharp, like the knives racked up in my father's kitchen.

'I tell him I have visa and I am studying here in a school but he just wants to ask about money. He takes my wallet and he wave my money in front of my face like a fan. "Is this all?" he says. "Do you expect her majesty government to pay for you when you come here?" I say I do not expect anything from his majesty's government except justice, fair play, these British things we hear so much about. This makes him cross. I tell him I have sponsor. You, Blake's. This make him more cross. He tells me I can go but to come back tomorrow because he will keep my passport and my papers because there is problem, he says. I ask again about my sister. My sister, he says, cannot come into the country. He tells me that she is already halfway back to Afghanistan. I do not know why this has happened. I have documents from your government.'

But there is a new member of the government. Pent. I can just imagine him checking every single passenger list, scanning for anyone who might be competition, anyone who he thinks he might be able to use in some way. 'You can't go back to Heathrow,' I say.

'Patroclus, of course he has to go back.'

'Minou is right. Ahmet has to go back.'

'You can't be serious! They'll put him on a plane, or detain him so he can't train, or so he can't even enter the races. You know what Pent is capable of...'

'We won't let that happen and he'll compete,' says Blake. 'And,' he turns to Ahmet, 'we'll have your twin sister back here in no time. I promise you, even if it means we have to borrow a jet and fly out there ourselves to get her.'

This makes Farsi raise an eyebrow and there's a shadow of a smile on his face. He probably thinks it's just a silly boast, well-meaning but nothing more than that. He doesn't know Blake. I look at Minou and she makes one of those 'here-we-go-again' faces. Borrowing a jet! I hope he intends to borrow a pilot, too; I don't fancy Blake sitting at the controls with an 'Idiot's Guide to Jet Flying' on his lap.

Blake, still in his friendly, well-meaning Percy mode, carries on reassuring Ahmet and then after a little while shows him to his room. When Blake comes back in, he is all business.

'Now, about tomorrow. Heathrow. Trokka, I think you should ride shotgun. Could you be Ahmet's lawyer? No, that won't do, will it?'

'No, it won't, not unless some legal firm employs

five-foot-three-inch thirteen-year-old lawyers!'

'Never mind, all you have to do is find out this man's extension number, this immigration officer. I'll pack you a bag of tricks and run through an idea I have. This man who interviewed Ahmet needs a mashing, I reckon, what do you say?'

We agree.

'He's a Pent toad, isn't he?' I ask.

'He's a Pent snake, and we're going to coil him into a gnarly knot!'

He makes it sound easy but of course it won't be, because nothing ever runs exactly to plan. That's the last rule.

Chapter 8

Heathrow.

Never been here before. Never been abroad, even. And now here we are at Heathrow. Through a tunnel and into something that looks like an upturned tub of Duplo – all higgledy-piggledy, tubes and blocks and glass and grey.

Terminal One, that's where Mr and Mrs Blake drop us, telling us to call them when we're through. Then they pull away and we're on our own in a jungle of wheely trolleys, baggage and hissing doors. I sling Blake's small bag of tricks over my shoulder, hoping I won't have to dip into it, and check that my mobile is on and Blake's number is up on the screen. I put it back in my pocket and just keep my hand resting on it, so it doesn't get knocked.

Zone A, Level Three, is where we have to go.

Immigration and Excise. It sounds like somewhere they cut you up. I don't say this to Ahmet though. I hope the phone operates from inside this building; that was one thing we didn't think about. My hand feels sweaty.

At 10.25 am exactly, the time of Ahmet's appointment, we find ourselves at the reception desk of Immigration and Excise, a pokey box of a room, with two men and one woman, all of them wearing short-sleeved white shirts and blue ties. Should I make contact with Blake now? No, wait.

Ahmet gives them the name of the officer he is due to see and they all look blank. 'Sorry, sir, can't help. Perhaps you could show us your passport, papers...'

But just at that moment another officer bustles in. Burly, hair a razor-cut stubble, bright red spots on his cheeks and a chin like a rugby ball. 'Yes?' he says curtly to us, ignoring his fellow immigration officials. Then, as if remembering, 'Oh, Mr Forsi, yes. Come this way.'

'His name is Farsi.'

'Who are you?' he says to me.

'My friend,' says Ahmet calmly. 'He will help with my English.'

One of the other officers glances up from his

paperwork, eyeing the officer like he's not seen him before, but he doesn't say anything, and nor do the other two.

'I see. All right, then.' He opens a side door and ushers us through into a long grey corridor. 'Follow me.'

He sets off at a brisk pace and we pass door after door, turn left, down stairs, along a landing with glass on one side that looks down onto the Arrivals concourse, with hundreds of travellers milling out into a sea of waiting friends and relations. Then our man stops, unlocks a door, no different to any of the other million doors we've passed, and tells us to go in and take a seat.

OK, the eagle has landed. We're here. I press Call. Give the mobile a couple of seconds to get through and ring at the other end and then switch it off. Blake will be ready now.

The room we're shown into is another grey box, a shoe box, nothing but a couple of chairs, desk, hook to hang a coat, fan on the ceiling. Where is the phone? Blake said there would be a phone. Do not panic, Patroclus. Think.

'Sit down, Mr Farsi and Mr Farsi's friend.'

'Excuse me,' I say. 'It might be necessary to make a phone call during this interview. Our lawyer said to ring if there was anything we didn't understand.'

'Oh, did he now? Won't be any need for that, I'm sure.'

'He said it was a legal obligation...'

The man scowls and mutters to himself. Then looks round the room as if he expects a phone to be hanging from the bare, plastic wall.

'This is not your office then,' I say politely.

'Course not. Interview room.'

'Oh? I didn't notice a number or name on the outside. Looks more like a broom cupboard,' I say politely. Well, as politely as I can manage. 'Though without the brooms in it, of course.'

The man ignores me and snaps open a drawer in the desk, slams it back and then opens a second one. 'Here.' He pulls out a phone, bangs it down. 'Right. Back in one moment.' And he marches out of the room, leaving the two of us on our own. Farsi raises an eyebrow but says nothing. Blake warned us not to talk if we were left alone, saying that they were bound to have recording devices tucked away somewhere, hoping to catch us out.

I peer through the crack in the half-open door, just to check he's not lurking outside. He's not, so I quickly step over to the desk and memorise the number and extension, but before I can text it through to Blake the man is back.

'Snooping round my desk, eh? I think you had better sit down, Mr...'

'Patroclus,' I say. 'I was just checking to see if your phone was plugged in. Our lawyer...'

'I've had quite enough about your lawyer,' he says. He sits and folds his hairy blunt fingers together on the desk and stares at me for a moment. 'So, we have another foreign body, as it were. I didn't have instructions about other foreign bodies, so if you don't mind, Mr Patrocolarse, you just keep your mouth shut. If you'd be so kind, of course.'

I sit, nudging my chair a little further away from Ahmet so that the man won't quite have me in his eyeline. Then, as soon as the questions start, I slip my hand into my pocket, and, praying that all my practising the night before will pay off, I text Blake the phone number, then an x, a 4, and a 3.

'I telephone my family in Kabul this morning,' Ahmet says. 'They tell me no plane comes in from London. So where is my sister? You did not do as you said.'

'Can't help that. Not my area. Too big a turn-around at this end. I'm the "meet and greet" department. That's what we call ourselves, makes us sound friendly.' He laughs and I catch a faint whiff of onion. 'My colleagues in "snatch and despatch" are a different crew altogether. And they aren't very good at communicating. Sorry about that, but I'm sure she'll turn up – just not in the UK, all right. Now, back to business. Your visa has a few question marks over it, I'm afraid, so what we'll do is get our little stamp...' He pulls out a stamp and ink box from his pocket, sniffs, whacks the stamp into the ink box, pulls Ahmet's passport from his other pocket and is just about to smack the stamp down, when the phone rings. For a split second he looks quite thrown as if he had forgotten about the phone being there, even after all our fussing. He picks it up and I can hear something like a high-pitched hornet swarm down the other end of the phone. Our rugby-chinned officer's red cheeks glow a little redder.

'Yes, of course, Minister... Right away, Minister... A mistake, you say... We... I mean I... No... No... No...' There are so many 'no's strung out one after the other, they make me think of supermarket sausages. I don't know why – tasteless and ugly I suppose.

He glares at us. Ahmet sits neatly, hands on knees. I wish I could hear what Blake is saying; he can do an unbeatable impression of Sir Pent. 'Right away, Sir, Minister. Yes. Yes.' And then as many yeses as there were nos. I hope Blake isn't overdoing it.

He motions for us to get up. A moment later he puts down the phone and then stands staring at it for about ten seconds. I know what he's thinking, he's thinking, how did Sir Pent know exactly which room he was in, when he didn't know it himself; when he didn't know there was a phone in there?

'Are we finished, then?' I ask.

'What?' He looks up, frowning. 'Oh, yes. That will be all.'

I pull open the door, but Ahmet hasn't moved. Time to go before the giant clunking penny clicks inside this bruiser's skull.

'And my sister, can you now tell me what has happened to her?'

'Er, not exactly.' He coughs. 'Not my department as I said, er, Mr Farsi. Here's your passport and papers.' He pushes them across the desk with one hand, and picks up the ink box and unused stamp with the other.

'Not your department?' Ahmet's voice is so cold it sounds like it's been chipped out of permafrost. I can see a vein throbbing at the side of his head. 'And what department is it that I try? Who is it that has taken her!'

'Don't get funny, sunshine...'

'I am not making the funny.'

The bruiser's about as heated as Ahmet is icy. I fear an explosion is imminent, and it won't do us any good at all.

I grab his arm. 'Ahmet! Time to go. We can speak to the Minister of Sport.' That at least checks the bruiser for a moment, long enough for us to exit. 'Keep walking and don't look back.' I have a tight grip on his arm in case he decides to about-turn and have another go. 'That man can't help. He's nothing,' I say. 'He's not real. He's a con.'

'Con?'

'Fake. Not real.' Out of the corner of my eye, through the long window that looks down onto Arrivals, I'm aware of a sudden change in the pattern of movement on the concourse. At first it makes me think of a shark moving into a shoal, but then I see it's just people moving back, allowing a path for a group of VIPs to sweep through. They're heading straight for the escalator to our level.

'Then who shall I be asking, Patroclus?' He stops, forcing me to stop, too.

'Blake,' I say. It's a bit feeble, but it's true. Blake is the one who always knows, who's got the contacts. 'The sooner we get back, the sooner we can do some serious checking. Trust me.'

'I trust you, Patroclus, and your friends. They are

good people but this is my sister, my twin. I cannot think without her. I cannot run. I must find her, you understand.'

Of course I believe him, even though I wouldn't mind sending *my* sister off to Kabul for a long holiday. 'I understand.'

There's a sudden flurry of flashing lights, a hubbub of voices, and men with cameras and microphones stepping backwards off the escalator just as we are trying to get by. And then a horribly familiar voice calls out: 'How splendid, such serendipity. The very man I have come to see, Ahmet Farsi.' And right in front of us is a velvet, plum-coloured Sir Pent, flanked by minders with shoulders like diving platforms, and eyes masked by square-framed dark glasses and those things in their ears that mean someone else is telling them what to do. Sharks don't have to think; they just bite. Sir Pent's hand comes down on Farsi's shoulder and he smiles for the cameras which pop and flicker. Not wanting to be recognised, I quickly step to one side and duck my head.

Ahmet is unfazed. 'You are minister I think,' he says. 'You can help me then.'

'Nothing I would like better, young man. Absolutely delighted.'

And the cavalcade sweeps by, leaving me standing by the top of the empty escalators, alone. I kick myself into gear and run after them, trying to push in, but one of the sharks in black grips my arm and, making sure that no photographer is looking our way, heaves me sideways, so I go skidding along the shiny floor until I'm almost back at the escalator.

Patroclus. Mission one. Failure. I reach for my mobile and call Blake.

Chapter 9

'Follow them.'

I try to explain to Blake that they're surrounded by security guards and press photographers, and that I've already been ejected with less ceremony than a garbage bag down a disposal chute.

'My Pimpernel pack, Trokka. Time to use it. Go to the nearest Gents and open it there, but be quick. Then get back on Pent's tail. Whatever you do, don't let Farsi get away.'

'Right.'

'Go!'

I go, running so fast on the slippy floor that my feet skid Tom-and-Jerry-style as I corner my way round into the Gents.

This is different to school and prefects and bullies and Bins; this is the outside; the grown world. Does

Blake – do any of us – know what we are really up against? Tricking a gorilla squeezed into a blue uniform is one thing; outsmarting Pent and a school of shark-like security men is something else. Maybe it's just me; I'm better at invisible, at anonymous, than at bearding the lion in his den – whatever that means.

I click the cubicle door shut.

The pack is pure Pimpernel: a pair of wire-rim glasses; a neat blue and white zip jacket with *Lycée Française* stitched in red loopy italics on its front; a press card on a cord to hang round my neck – the photo taken and printed last night is me wearing the wire-rim glasses and sporting a crop of surfer-bleached hair; and the last item, wrapped in tissue paper. You've guessed it: a wig. I shuffle it on my head and snap on the jacket and glasses. Give myself a check in the mirror. I'm me, not me. Adjust the wig. Look at my name on the pass: Armand St Juste – sounds like something my sister drinks at breakfast – but French. Why French? French is my worst subject at school. I pull a face. Trust Blake to land me in it.

I bolt out of the Gents.

I find them in the VIP lounge with a proper press conference in full swing. There's a table with Sir Pent sitting in the middle. To his right are three young runners – Ahmet and two others who must have just flown in for the Internationals in Cambridge. I recognise them both: big names on the junior circuit, Rodriguez Martin from Mexico and, my heart sinks, Philippe Luis from France. My luck.

The men in black are at either end of the table and also scattered through the crowd of journalists and stray members of the public who've maybe forgotten that they have planes or trains to catch, drawn moth-like to this bubble of activity because there is a TV crew filming. I hitch up my shoulder bag, take out a pen and notebook and edge my way in.

'It's my pleasure, of course, to welcome such talented youngsters to the UK...'

Why? Why's he smarming up to these guys? They're not going to run for him.

'They will all be guests at our brand-new sporting academy. The best of everything...'

That's it! The SIRP Academy. That man at the race, old boot-polish, even tried to get me to sign up. What goes on there? Secret experiments, brain-washing? Nothing good, that's for sure.

'Minister, St Juste,' I blurt out in what I hope is a French accent, 'Lycée Française. Do all the runners have to stay at the Academy?' And before he can answer, I say, 'Isn't it owned...' I can feel the TV camera swinging my way and the lights heating up my face, making me sweat, and I have a sudden panic that my wig will start to slip, '...by SIRP, a company in which you have a controlling interest?'

Sir Pent's face twitches. 'Ridiculous!' he snaps. 'Next question, please.' I see Farsi looking my way, slightly puzzled. Philippe Luis's eyebrows have shot up in amused surprise. I guess my pretend French accent is more pretend than French. Too late now: I plunge on. 'Minister, can you assure us that all the international competitors are being welcomed, a word you used a moment ago, into this country?'

'Of course! Ridiculous question! Do I know you?'

He most certainly does. My ex-headmaster has me partly to blame for his brief stay in prison. I keep going: 'Can you promise us that none of them are going to be detained by the immigration department,' I pause to check that the camera gets the full force of this, and then let him have it, 'as Ahmet Farsi was just ten or twenty minutes ago?'

I can hear the intake of breath. Sir Pent's pale cheeks looks sticky and yellow, his eyes like lasers; he'd sizzle me if he could. Ahmet is looking puzzled, and then I catch just a hint of a smile. He didn't know who I was at all, not till now. So, my disguise passes muster; not bad, Trokka. And I know this is good TV; everybody loves a minister being grilled in public: one toasted minister and chips coming up. Can I really do it now, right now? Scupper Sir Pent before he does any real damage? Because I am one hundred per cent sure that he's up to his snaky eyeballs in a crooked scheme. Just one more question and then maybe journalists here will take over and finish him off. What if between us we get him to resign?

A tiny voice in my ear whispers: watch it, Trokka, pride before a fall. But it's too late, I'm on a roll. 'Minister, can you assure us that all these young runners are free to come and go as they like, that you are not keeping any of them against their will?'

Pent seems to shiver and then he explodes. He bangs his hand down so hard on the table that the microphone in front of him gives a massive *pop!* and totters over onto the floor. 'This is an outrage!' he screams. 'These are lies! You! Who are you working for?'

And then, jabbing his finger in my direction as if it were a skewer, he grabs the lapel of the security shark who was leaning over him, waiting for instructions. I can't hear what his orders are because there's chaos but it doesn't take a genius to figure out he wants me kebabed.

Journalists are shouting, the cameras are moving in for close-ups on Pent, and the members of the public who only stopped by out of idle curiosity are getting shoved and pushed one way and another. It's panic time.

I should have listened to the voice, shouldn't I, because this isn't quite what I intended. I tell myself that they can't arrest me, surely, not for asking questions. No. But who is going to look pretty silly when it turns out that Armand St Juste is Michael Patroclus from Peasely, and he's carrying a fake press pass? Me.

I clock the remaining men in black, fingers on their earpieces, their dark glasses all swivelling in my direction. I have two seconds. I see Ahmet jump to his feet. 'It is true!' he shouts. 'It is true!' There is a momentary lull and I take the opportunity to slither back through the press. 'This man is not good man. He know something about my sister and make promise that he do me favour. I do not want favour, I want my sister!'

Another even louder eruption, more shoving. I see a fist bunching and Ahmet ducking; the Mexican runner makes a break for it. 'Ahmet!' I yell and then,

'Now! Go!' I don't have time to check whether he understands that means get to the meeting place in double-quick time because a man in black has his long arm stretched past a big-bellied couple, both wearing rumpled Honolulu shorts and scarlet vests.

'Gotcha!'

I catch a glimpse of his square-cut face...but luckily escape is one thing I am skilled at. In one movement I've peeled myself out of the jacket and dropped down onto my hands and knees. Half a second to rip off my wig and glasses and stuff them into my shoulder bag and then I'm off on all fours, threading my way through a forest of legs. A couple of bruises later, I pop my head out from the scrum. I don't waste time looking to see if the black suit holding my jacket has managed to follow me, I just bolt straight back down the corridor away from the riot.

'There!' Someone shouts.

I glance back, giving them a chance to see I am not Armand the pint-sized French surfer. I can't tell whether the ploy makes any difference. There are two security sharks, one gesticulating, but not running after me; the other holding a phone to his mouth.

Skid round the corner. Lift and escalator. Which

one? A group of airport security guards are coming up the escalator, two steps at a time; the lift door opens. I jump in. It's empty, good. Going down. I scrabble in the bag and pull out the other bits Blake has put in. Gold chain, baseball cap. Genius. I put the cap on at a crazy tilt, hang the chain round my neck. Bling. And shiny tracksuit bottoms, too. I manage to haul them on over my jeans just as the door slides open. Deep breath and then, trying to model myself on all the rappers I've ever seen on MTV, I slope slowly out of the lift, nodding as if I'm listening to music, and walk straight by two security guards. They peer past me looking, I guess, for Mr Armand St Juste. Unlucky them.

I try not to hurry but I feel a horrid tightness right in the middle of my back, as if someone has their sights trained on me.

Keep going. Keep going.

No shouts, just crowds of travellers milling around.

Exit in sight. I pull out my mobile and call the car.

'We'll be there in a jiffy,' says Mr Blake. I don't think he quite realises the urgency.

I glance back towards the escalators. There's a shadow of black-suited sharks gazing down onto the concourse, their heads slowly moving one way then the other, scanning. I shift back into the doorway of a record store. 'Two minutes,' I say.

'We're almost there, Michael.'

A party of noisy Spanish teenagers swirl by and I hook up with them, peeling off just as I get to the exit. There's the limousine. Door opens and I jump in. At the same moment I see Ahmet charging out from an exit fifty yards further along. 'There he is!'

We manage to scoop him up.

'They were looking for you, Patroclus,' he says. He seems totally unruffled. 'But you have many disguises. Why is this?'

I slump back in the seat, exhausted. 'I think maybe Percy Blake should explain,' I say. 'It's something to do with his family and,' I take off my baseball cap, 'this.' I show him the little red flower stitched into the rim.

'What is this?' he asks.

I've said too much.

Chapter 10

'Why you show me this flower? Is it like brand for Blake company?'

Backtrack, Patroclus. 'No, not really.' I'm twisted round looking out through the rear window – I seem to spend half my life doing this – and, sure enough, just as we take the corner there's a sudden flurry of men piling out onto the pavement. I reckon they're too late to get the licence plate, though, so maybe we're safe. 'It's something called a Pimpernel,' I tell him. 'The sign is used by...' How do I explain without giving it all away? '...used by someone who helps out the Blakes sometimes.'

'Who is he, this Pimpernel? That man, that government man, that lying man, he use this word, too. He try to tell me that it is this flower take my sister! He promise if I come to his Academy with these other runners, he find my sister for me.'

What a liar! 'Listen, Ahmet, Pent is evil. You cannot believe anything he says.'

Ahmet waves away my words. 'He is nothing. He is liar. I know this. He is politician. How can flower take my sister. He think because I come from Afghanistan I know nothing. Tell me about this Pimpernel.'

As the motorway peels away beneath us, I try to explain what the Pimpernel is. It might not even be one person, I say, more like an organisation. A gang. To fight against bad people.

'Superman,' says Ahmet. 'Batman. Silver Surfer. We have this comix too, Michael, but they are not the real world.'

'Pimpernel is real.'

'You know him?'

And, like Pent, I lie. 'No, not exactly.'

'But he give you this hat!' He laughs but there is something steely and angry underneath. 'You did me a good service, Michael. I do not ever forget this. You show everyone on television how that man lies. The officer, immigration man, work for him. He get me to the airport to trap me. They want me to work for them. That man, Pent, he knows what happen to my sister. I think he take people he want to use and he squeeze them.'

He's not wrong about that.

'Blake will help you find your sister. You can count on that.'

'Blake? Why not Pimpernel?'

I don't answer that.

'Blake are very nice family but,' he laughs again, and then lowers his voice, 'they are silly people, no? Rich but silly. This is why you are friends with him, because he is rich.'

'No.' How do I say this without giving the game away? 'They're good people, just different. Trust me. If they say they can help, they will. They have loads of connections, you know, around the world.'

'Good.' He closes his eyes and leans his head back. 'Maybe they help but I will not run. I cannot, not till Soroya is safe.'

'But this is why you're here! You're the best! You can't just stop...'

He doesn't open his eyes. 'You can run Michael. I see you today; you are very fast. Down the passage, around the corner. *Pfft*. You change very fast, too. Three people today. One, two, three. Maybe you are Pimpernel.'

'Me! No.'

After a pause; 'You run as fast as you change,

Michael, and you will run faster than me. Maybe one day I will run in your shadow.'

I'm about to tell him that he can't talk like this when Blake senior flicks the intercom switch and says, 'Car on our tail. Looks a bit official.'

I peer back through the rear window. It's there, breathing down our exhaust. I can see the driver and the man beside him. Like cardboard cutouts. No expression. Then, as I watch, the driver leans forwards slightly, and maybe flicks a switch because the whirly light on the car's roof begins to spin and the siren wails like a howler monkey.

How did they trace this car?

'I'm going to have to stop,' says Mr Blake. He glances at Mrs Blake, who nods in agreement. We slow down and pull onto the hard shoulder. The other car swoops in front of us, blocking us from changing our minds, I suppose. I strip off my tracksuit bottoms, snatch the cap back from Ahmet and shove them both under the seat. Nothing to do now but sit back and wait.

The driver comes over – so he's not cardboard after all. His passenger stays in the car, watching, talking on a phone. There's no marking on the car, and neither of them are in uniform, which I can't help thinking is a bit odd.

A rap on the glass. I see Mrs Blake resting her hand on her husband's arm and I hear her murmur, '*Cochons sales, mon cheri*.'

'Of course they are, m'dear.'

What their driver doesn't notice, but I do, is Mrs Blake discreetly leaning forwards and pressing a switch on the dashboard. A little red light comes on and blinks when the man starts to speak. They're recording him! The Blakes, Mr and Mrs, are not quite so goofy as they seem.

'Who's the owner of this vehicle?'

'Well, I am of course!'

'You're in a chauffeur's uniform.'

'Yes,' Mr Blake puts on his extra-drawling voice, 'splendid, isn't it?'

The officer, if that's what he is, doesn't let us know whether he thinks it is splendid or not. He has a stony face behind dark glasses. He also has a little silver 'S' on his black tie. S for what? Not secret service, that's for sure.

'Papers. Licence.' He leans through the window, looking back at the two of us. 'Who are these then, eh?'

'Guests of mine...'

'Look like illegal immigrants to me. You two, got passports, have you?'

Ahmet already has his in his hand and starts to hold it out to the man but I stop him. The old penny finally clicks. 'Wait a minute, Ahmet. Who are you?' I say to the man. 'Are you are a police officer, or what?'

'Can we see identification, officer?' says Mr Blake. 'If you don't mind, of course.'

The man ignores Mr Blake. 'What did you say, sonny?' He peers at me. 'Is there a Frenchie in here, Armand St Juste?' He pronounces it 'juiced'. 'You wouldn't be him, would you?'

'You don't have any identification, do you? You're not a police officer. You work for SIRP.' There's not a flicker out of him, but I bet I'm right. I know I am.

'Well, well,' he says, 'who've we got here, a regular Inspector Morse.' And then to Ahmet. 'Nice tan. Been on holiday, have you?'

Ahmet says nothing.

Mrs Blake tuts loudly, plucks a mobile phone from her handbag and to my surprise taps in a number and starts to speak: 'Black Mondeo, registration AS21 EAN... *Bien sûr*, I understand. You are sure? No police vehicle of that registration? Thank you.' She clicks off the phone. '*Cheri*, tell this *cochon* to move his car or we report him to the real police.'

'No need for any of that,' says the man. 'Just a routine check.'

'I think you should do as she says,' says Mr Blake, and touches a button to close the window.

'Just one thing,' says the man, gripping the window and stopping it from closing. 'You tell your employer, grandad, that there is an investigation into his business practice. All right?' I can see his fingers whiten where they're pressing the top of the window. There's a thin squeal coming from inside the doorframe – the electric motor for the window. 'Espionage,' he says. 'That sort of thing. People dressing up, you know, like this Mr Juiced. Oh, and there's a nasty little snitch called Pimpy Nell. There's been trouble with him and all. As for the tourist here,' says the man, turning his stone-face towards Ahmet, 'the Minister's very interested in you. Your progress, know what I mean? He recommends you have a good think about his offer.'

None of us say anything but I wonder what Pent has in mind; Ahmet would be better off making a deal with a tarantula, but now's not the time to tell him.

The SIRP agent releases the window. 'Have a nice day,' he adds, as it slides closed. Mr Blake puts the car into gear and pulls carefully out onto the road again. The man watches us, his face still blank under the mask of his dark glasses. Sharks don't show any expression either, but I see that his companion, who's been sitting in their car the whole time, does that silly pistol thing with his right hand as we pass him.

'There are mans like that in Kabul,' says Ahmet, bleakly. 'They can take your car, take your house. Thiefs, you know, but no one stop them, not soldiers, not police, no one. I did not think it would be like that here.'

No, I don't think we did, either.

'Such a man,' says Mrs Blake. 'He eats too much meat, I think. Did you smell him, *cheri*? McDonald's.'

'I did. A total bounder, I'd say. Now home James, isn't that right, my dear?'

'Jiggedy jig.'

They both laugh as if they've said something funny.

I don't like to remind them that neither of us are called James. I wonder whether Ahmet is going to tell us what this offer is that Pent put to him, but he doesn't. After a little while, I ask him.

He shrugs and pulls a face but doesn't answer. As if the whole notion is not serious. Instead he says: 'You say Percy Blake will find Soroya?'

'Your sister? Yes, of course.' He will too.

'OK.' He closes his eyes and leans his head back. 'Do you know what twin is, Michael?'

'Yes, I know.'

He shakes his head. 'No one knows, except maybe this man, Sir Pent. It is half myself, Michael. She is half myself. If she is lost, I am lost too.'

Chapter 11

We reach the Blake house at ten that evening. The electric gate swings open and Mr Blake drives slowly in, the wheels crunching on the gravel. The house is lit up like an ocean liner, lights blazing from every window. And I find myself wondering what Blake and the Geek have been up to while Ahmet and I have been playing Tom and Jerry in Terminal One.

'There we are now.' Mr Blake switches off the engine and opens his door. 'You staying here tonight, Michael?'

'Yes, if that's all right, Mr Blake. I told my parents I would be.'

'Of course. Splendid.'

Their dog, an old golden retriever, lifts his head from his paws and then walks stiffly up to the car.

'Hello, Burton,' says Mr Blake. The dog sniffs his

hand and yawns. Mr Blake pats his head and then to me and Ahmet he says, 'Famished? Yes? Food I think.' He talks a bit like a postcard. I don't think he and my dad could ever hold a conversation, not in a million years.

'Yes, thank you, Mr Blake and Mrs Blake,' says Ahmet politely. 'You are very kind, taking me to London for this meeting about my passport and my sister.'

'Nonsense. We like a spin in the motor, don't we Isabelle?'

Mrs Blake smiles but says nothing. Neither mention the incident on the road; it's impossible to tell what they think about anything. I wonder if they even talk to Blake about Pimpernel business.

'Come on, m'dear,' he says, taking his wife's arm. His parting shot as they go into the house is: 'She's French, you know. Terrible cook. Sandwiches all right?'

The gate clicks shut. Beyond the pool of light shed by the house the garden is full of lumpy black shapes, heavy-shouldered giants like the ones in my father's stories.

Ahmet, like me, is standing by the car, both of us taken up with our own thoughts.

'We do not have such things in my home.' At first

I think he's talking about sandwiches, or maybe the shapes, but then I realise he means the automatic security gate.

'Me neither.'

'No?' He seems surprised. 'I think all Percy's friends are rich. With house like this.'

'Rich! You're joking.'

Burton, perhaps remembering that he's meant to be a guard dog, walks over to the gate and gives a couple of experimental growls, and then does his stiff-leg walk back to his bed on the porch.

'Roses,' says Ahmet quietly. 'Can you smell them? This we have at home. Many.' It's true, the air is thick with their musky smell. 'Even with the war, they are still growing. Beautiful and ugly things together.'

'What are you thinking, Ahmet?'

The porch intruder light goes off. I can only just make out the whiteness of his eyes, nothing else.

'Is this safe here, Patroclus, this place?'

Safe? What's safe? Sir Pent is on the move. There've been break ins at the factories and SIRP agents pulling us over on the road, faking it up as immigration officials, threatening and bullying. It doesn't matter that Pent still doesn't know who the Pimpernel is, it's the Blakes and their business that he's after. One old dog and a set of electronic gates won't stop Sir Pent, but then Blake will have thought of something. Probably what he's been doing all day. 'We'll be all right,' I say. 'Come on, Ahmet. Let's go in.'

Forget safe – the inside of the house is in chaos, like it's had a visit from troupe of jitterbugging chimpanzees.

Mess everywhere. Scrumpled-up drawings and sketches. A toxic stink of glue and paint and I don't know what. And terrible music pumping out of the speakers: brass bands and bagpipes. And there's Blake, like a cross between a mad professor and the hunchback of Notre Dame, bleached hair spiked out, and wearing the glasses with the super-thick lenses that I know he doesn't need. He's up on a stepladder adding scribbles to a pad he has pinned up by the light.

'Ultimulta!' cries Blake when he spots us coming. 'Look and marvel at my genius! Total ultimulta.' And why is he pretending to be Italian, or does he think he sounds Greek? I think I prefer the fake surf-speak. 'Ultimulta'! Even my father wouldn't come up with such a stupid word. 'You have to tell me everything. Everything! But first: grab your eyeballs, my little grommies, and marvel!' He swings his arm dramatically and points at the table up at the far end of the room. There, practically as big as the fireplace behind the table, are a pair of giant, and I mean *huge*, blood-red and ice-white runners. 'Are they not total bombies!'

I spoke too soon. 'What's a bombie, Blake?'

'A big wave, Trokka. A big, perfect wave.'

'And who's the giant grommie who's going to fit into your bombies, Blake?'

'Oh, Trokka, Trokka the mocker!' And he does his high-pitched giggle.

Ahmet catches my eye and pulls a face. I know what he's saying: 'How can I believe that this boy can really help? He's crazy.'

Blake? Maybe, a bit – but a bit of a genius, too. And, at this time of night, a bit annoying. The giggle and silly made-up words don't usually bother me, especially when he's pulling the wool over the eyes of some dim Bin, but with Ahmet, it's sort of different. Ahmet is maybe the best young athlete in the world, a hero, and we're helping him, or trying to, so the pretending feels funny. But rules are rules. Nobody can ever know who the Pimpernel is. Nobody. Not even our friends.

'Where's Minou?'

'Oh, busy,' he says airily. 'Tell you later.'

Ahmet is walking round the giant runners. They look so weird, like they've just been beamed down from out of space.

'What do you think?' asks Blake.

'Extraordinary,' he says. 'Did you make these in one day, Percy?'

'Mm? Oh, yes.'

I touch the fabric to see whether they're real, or just mocked up with something like papier-mâché. They're real, all right. Funny little omissions though: no rubber reinforcement at the front, or the usual leather or stronger material to help keep the shape. But when I lift one, I'm surprised at how light it is. In a real size it would be like air. 'Good,' I say. 'I don't suppose you have a pair that Ahmet or I could actually run in?'

'Not yet.'

'Not built to last, are they?' I say.

'No. One race only. But they will be dynamite, Trokka. Take my word for it.' He's grinning like a donkey dipped in retsina.

'You're not serious?' I have a sudden worry that he really has devised an exploding runner.

He winks. Ahmet has his back to us. I pull a face. Insane! Explosives in a pair of running shoes? He can't mean it!

Blake takes off his glasses and lifts one eyebrow as if he's expecting me to figure something out.

Then the penny drops. At least I think it does. SIRP are after the latest Blake runners. That's what all the robberies have been about. So now Blake wants them to steal this giant pair, his Trojan shoe. But then what? SIRP sneak them off to their factory and the factory blows up! What good will that do? Clever, maybe, but still criminal.

'You can't,' I say. If Minou were here she would never let him do anything criminal.

'Oh?'

Ahmet looks from one to the other of us, not understanding. And just as well. I don't know much about what's happening in his country but he'll have seen things we've never even imagined. Bombs. Horrors.

'You just have to trust me, Trokka.' Then he says it again in a silly voice, but his eyes are pale and serious.

And I nod because although he's a bit crazy, I know he wouldn't do anything really dangerous. He just wouldn't. The trouble is I'm so fuzzy with tiredness that I can't figure out what he really intends. I wish the Geek was here. 'Where is Minou? You haven't said.'

'No... I tell you what...' But he doesn't because Ahmet, who has picked up one of the giant shoes and is studying it closely, says, 'This is prototype?'

'Not quite. Close. Nearly there. Just some figures and plans. I've still got to tidy up the loose ends. But it's a bit hush-hush. You understand, don't you?'

Ahmet nods. 'Of course. Secret. I understand.'

'Now.' Blake claps his hands together. 'Sit down. Full report and protein.' He beams. 'Ahmet, you look totally axed, if you don't mind me saying so.'

Blake still hasn't answered my question.

Ahmet sits in the chair Blake pulls out for him and smiles politely. Blake leaves the room.

If Ahmet doesn't know what 'totally axed' means, he doesn't say. In fact, he doesn't give much away at all, our Ahmet; but I can see he's been watching Blake, maybe trying to make up his mind about him. And why not? Thousands of miles from home; his twin sister deported, maybe kidnapped; his host, a barmy inventor and me, what does he make of me? A nippy runner and quick-change artist?

Well, at least I got him out of that snake-pit interview room and showed Pent up for the fraud monster he is. He knows Blake and I are not enemies; the trouble is, how useful are we as friends?

Pent still has the power. I bet that's what's going round our Ahmet's mind: who will get his sister back, SIRP or Blake? Well, he'll have to work that one out for himself. Meanwhile I want to jostle some information out of Percy Blake.

'I'll give Percy a hand,' I say to Ahmet.

Out in the kitchen I grab his arm. 'Blake! What is going on? Where's Minou? You haven't told me. In fact, Blake, you haven't told me anything.'

'You're right, Patroclus, but food first.'

'No! Those shoes. Are they explosive?'

'Did I say that?'

'Blake! You said "dynamite", so do you mean they're like a booby trap, an explosive one?'

'No. Of course not. You should know me better than that.'

'Sorry.' He's right – except isn't he the one who keeps himself hidden away, even from his closest friends?

'I'll tell you about Minou in two seconds,' he says. 'Let's sort Ahmet out first. He looks like he doesn't know which way's up.'

'He's smarter than you think.'

'Is he? That's not what I meant, though. Here, take this.' He thrusts a tray stacked with sandwiches into my hand while he wheels a trolley with a jug of hot chocolate and a bowl of fruit on it through into the other room. Mr and Mrs Blake come in. Mrs Blake says something in French and hands Blake a CD. Of course, it's the recording of when the SIRP man stopped us. They both say good night and then, once they have gone, Blake insists we give him a report of the day. I do that. He makes no comment but puts the CD into a player and we listen. It's all clear as a bell so when Blake says, 'Nothing that's really incriminating', I'm astonished.

'He was threatening us!'

'Yes, of course. I can hear that. But there's nothing that proves he works for SIRP. Sorry, but it wouldn't wash in a court of law.'

'Wash?' asks Ahmet. He's been sipping his hot chocolate while we listened to the recording, though I noticed that all the time he was watching Blake.

'Not good evidence,' says Blake.

'You know about lawyers?' Ahmet is surprised.

Blake laughs. 'Family's always up to its armpits in lawyers.' And then without a pause he says, 'Did Sir Pent offer you a deal?'

Ahmet doesn't seem particularly surprised by the question. 'Work for him, yes. Be sponsored by him, by his SIRP company, you know.'

'And if you do?'

'My sister. He promise he give her visa. Let her stay. No problem.'

'Even though she's no longer in the country.'

'He say he knows where she is.'

'Do you know where she is, then?'

'Of course no.' For the first time, Ahmet sounds cross. 'If I know where she is, I go to her. Simple, yes.'

'Yes, of course. But you came back here with Michael, and you didn't have to.'

'Michael say you will find my sister.'

'And you trust Michael?'

Ahmet shrugs and makes an expressive gesture with both hands as if to say, 'How do I know who to trust?'

'Well, we've done our homework, Ahmet. Minou is in France because that is where your sister is. Did Pent tell you that? No. Though I'm pretty certain he authorised it. Flight BA201. Someone on the shop floor gave us the passenger list. The captain has done business with Blake's before – helping with a quick exit, that sort of thing. Told me she was escorted out of Orly Airport near Paris. Thought it was by the French secret police but wasn't too sure. Minou tracked them to the Gare du Nord but then lost the trail. So she's somewhere in northern France. Near the coast, that's my bet. Minou is on her way back,' he says to me. 'She'll be here in the morning.'

I'm impressed. I glance at Ahmet, expecting him to look pleased that we've made this much progress, but he looks like someone who's had all hope vacuumed out of them.

'They can't keep Soroya; her papers are in order! How can they do this?'

'This has got nothing to do with papers and passports. This is kidnap, Ahmet.' His voice is sympathetic but behind his goofy, fake specs his eyes gleam with excitement. 'Minister Pent doesn't seem to think laws have anything to do with him, but he's going to get drilled for this. He'll go down for good.'

'But first we find Soroya.'

'Of course we'll get her back. That's number one, numero uno.' He pushes his glasses up his nose a bit. 'And I know just the man to help.'

'It is this Pimpernel?' says Ahmet.

Blake gives his high, excited laugh and claps his hands together. 'The very man. How did you guess?'

Ahmet shrugs. 'And you know how to find this Pimpernel?'

Strange thing is, I saw this question coming, but I don't think Blake did because his expression flickers, the mask of excitable Percy Blake, wannabe surfer and boffin inventor, slipping for an instant, but then he blinks and gives a sheepish grin. 'Oh, not really. He just gets in touch, you know. Funny old fish.'

'Fish?'

'Just an expression.'

'Yes.' Ahmet sounds flatter and colder than a year-old pancake. 'But you think you can bring Soroya back here. How old are you, Percy? How old is Minou, Patroclus? Thirteen maybe. Are you child, still?'

'Well, technically yes, I suppose...'

'In my country, children do what grown-ups say. What parents tell them. But you think you can do this thing, bring my sister to me, even with powerful man like this Mr Pent...'

Blake looks him straight in the eye. 'Trust me,' he says, for the third time this evening, I note.

'Of course. Your family is kind to me.' He gets up. 'My race tomorrow. Maybe I should sleep. You too, Michael. More running, yes?' He smiles suddenly. I like him but he makes me feel sad. It's as if he's just beyond our reach. Maybe we can't help him.

After he's gone I say, 'Do you think we'll be able to rescue his sister?'

'Isn't that what the Pimpernel's for?' He smiles, the real smile, the real him, the him I trust.

'And these new *dynamite* running shoes?'

'Don't worry about them. It's not what you think. Go to bed, because you're going to need your wits about you tomorrow. Pent is bound to try and get his claws into Ahmet again, and it'll happen at the race.'

I say good night and go to bed. I'm sharing a room with Ahmet but he already seems to be asleep by the time I've washed. The room's dark. I don't put on a light, just get into bed and then I'm out. That's me. Simple. Close my eyes and it's sleep, deep and black as Blake's ocean.

Chapter 12

I don't know what wakes me but my eyes are wide open, looking up at the little circle of greenish light on the ceiling, a reflection from the alarm clock. It's not time to get up, too dark.

Silence, thick as a blanket. When I'm at home silence just means my dad isn't talking. There the night is full of little sounds, a squeak in the pipes, a murmur from machines in the kitchen, but this is different. Here, there's nothing.

I turn my head and see that Ahmet's bed is empty. That's what's different – there's not even the sound of his breathing in the room. Just gone to the bathroom, is what I presume, and I turn over and try to go back to sleep. But for some reason I can't. Time passes. The green numbers on the digital clock read 1.05...1.06...1.07...

I slip out of bed and, without turning on the light, I go to the door. Our room is on the ground floor, at the back of the house. A corridor leads along to the kitchen. There are three rooms on the other side of the corridor, Blake's bedroom and two workrooms. The doors are all shut and there's no light showing under them either. But there is a single light on at the end of the corridor, and the door into the kitchen is ajar. Maybe Ahmet is getting a drink of water. But something tells me that this isn't the case.

I slip down the corridor and gently push open the kitchen door. No light there but the door into the front room is also slightly open. Not a sound. No murmur of voices. I feel like a ghost.

I hesitate. Where is he? What is he doing?

Something is not right.

I hold my breath and move past the table and chairs and then freeze. A light comes on in the front room and I hear a voice, very soft, and another, sharper, as if startled. Ahmet and Blake?

I take two steps to the door and peer through the crack. Ahmet is standing by the mock running shoe and is half turned towards an armchair. Must be Blake sitting in it, though I can't see.

I can't hear what they're saying and I don't want to butt in so I decide to leave it and let them explain in the morning. I go back and climb into bed. I hear Ahmet returning a few minutes later. He stands quietly by the door as if to check whether I'm asleep or not. Again, I don't know why, but I don't want him to know that I'm awake, that I've been checking on him. I let myself breathe a little more loudly than normal, but even and steady. Of course I don't know if that's what I sound like when I'm sleeping, but it seems to work because moments later I hear him climbing into his bed and then there is silence again.

Strange. What were the two of them up to?

I must have fallen asleep because the next thing that happens is I hear the sharp crack of glass breaking, and the scuffle of feet on gravel.

The clock reads 4.22.

Out of bed. Spin round. Ahmet? No, he's there. Fast asleep it seems. Then a repeat of what I did before. Corridor. Kitchen. Pause. Noises. A curse.

Thieves!

I scrabble on the sideboard for something heavy I can use as a club. Rolling pin. Perfect. And what's this? A cheeseboard with a handle. Yes! Sword and shield. Patroclus. Warrior.

What about my rules?

Don't be noticed.

Stay invisible.

But I suppose something has changed in me because I don't hesitate. I push open the door and see a figure in the process of trying to manhandle Blake's giant shoe out through the broken window – but it won't quite fit and instead of trying to get out of the door, or shifting the way he's holding the shoe, the burglar keeps jabbing the shoe at the broken edges of glass, trying to make the gap bigger. An idiot. And I know exactly who it is, too. It's one of Jaco's Bins, the Maggot. Huge. Grabber hands but brains the size of a marble.

I don't know what I yell, something like 'AIEEEE!' I think. That's what Blake told me later. He said it was bloodcurdling. It has the effect of sending the Maggot into a frenzy and he suddenly pops through the window like a cork out of a bottle before I'm even halfway across the room.

I can't think why I haven't called for help or got Blake up but my blood's boiling and I'm just so angry with Pent and everything he's doing: all that oozing up to Ahmet when he's kidnapped his sister and then the cheating and thieving. And now it's right where we're sleeping. What next? Breaking into the café? Or into the Geek's flat? Threatening her. Her mum. My parents... They would do anything. It's too much. So I charge, and I would have caught him too, caught him red-handed. In my mind I'm Brad Pitt in *Troy*. The Maggot won't have a chance.

Dream on, Patroclus.

Halfway across the room something slams into the back of my knees and I crash face-first into the long leather sofa.

I hear a final yelp. The Maggot cutting himself on the window I expect. Then a familiar voice. 'Trokka! It looks like we've been attacked by a party of Apaches.'

I scrabble up and face Blake, who is wearing a giant Thomas the Tank Engine T-shirt and shorts. 'Blake! They've got your shoe! One of the Bins, Maggot...'

'I know.' He grabs my arm to stop me clambering through the window after our thief. 'Watch.'

The intruder light is on and I can see the Maggot half-hopping half-running across the gravel to the gate, the giant shoe clutched in front of his face so he can't see properly. There is a flash of brighter light, and then another.

'Camera,' says Blake.

The Maggot runs straight into a bush, reels back, peers round the shoe, spots the gate, hurls the shoe over it and clumsily hauls himself up onto it. Another flash catches the Maggot panic-stricken, staring back at the house. And then he drops down the other side. Scoops up the shoe. There is the sound of a motor.

'You're letting him go!'

'Of course. It's all on camera, Trokka.'

An engine roars. There's the squeal of tyres and the flash of the vehicle passing in front of the gate.

And I call the Maggot dim! I feel my cheeks get oven-hot. Thank goodness it's dark. 'Sorry, Blake. I forgot. It's the Trojan shoe. You wanted it stolen.'

'Don't worry, Trokka, you were great, totally stoked. You would've terrified the lights out of me. I hoped you'd do something warlike. It'll pull the wool over their Trojan eyes, Trokka. And now I've plenty of evidence against our thief. Not that he's important; it's Pent we want.'

'Pent is never going to do anything as stupid as breaking and entering.'

Blake laughs. 'I know he's not, but where do you think the shoe is going?'

'To him?'

'Exactly.'

'But we won't have any evidence of that, will we?'

'I think we might. Let me show you something.'

We go back to his workroom, pausing outside my room just to see if there's any stirring from Ahmet.

There isn't. Blake raises his eyebrows. 'Heavy sleeper,' he murmurs.

I'm not sure if he's being serious or not. Of course, he doesn't know that I spied on Ahmet when he was up earlier. I leave it and don't say anything for the moment.

We go into Blake's room. He flicks on the light and fires up his desktop computer. Hits a couple of command keys and the screen is suddenly alive, blurry images in slashes of grey and black. 'No colour at the moment, but it'll be clearer in the morning.'

I'm looking closely at the screen. I can make out the back of someone's head and the side of someone else's face. Maggot. And Jaco, I think. And someone else, I don't know who. Adult. With slick black hair, like a shiny pot... The man from SIRP with the greasy voice!

'You've got a camera in the shoe!'

'Yes. Neat, isn't it. Need a bit of luck of course. But who knows, we should get Sir Pent himself.'

'Blake, this is genius.'

'Glad you like it, Trokka.' He grins.

The Patroclus brain is getting into gear. 'And does the camera pick up sound, too?'

'Yes, but it won't be good in the van. We'll check

it later. It's on continuous film mode. I've tweaked the battery so it'll last for a while.'

'This could do for him.'

Blake pulls a face. 'It's possible. I mean, that's the plan, but he's in a strong position and getting stronger. I don't know. We've got plenty to do yet.'

'Ahmet's sister.'

'Yes. And Ahmet, too.'

'What do you mean? He's here. Safe.'

'Well, I don't know about safe.'

'You think Pent wants him that much?'

'A runner as good as Ahmet, of course he wants him. The question is, has he got him already?'

'But he's here, asleep in his bed. What are you talking about?'

'Maybe Pent's "got" him because Pent has "got" his sister.' Blake swings his chair round to face me. 'How did they know about the new shoe? I only devised it today, and yet here they are. Bit of a coincidence.'

I think about it. 'I'm sure Ahmet doesn't trust Pent, but he *was* very interested in the prototype shoe.'

'Wasn't he? He was even up in the night...'

'I know.'

Blake raises an eyebrow. 'That's pretty good, Trokka. I didn't hear you at all. Where were you?'

'In the kitchen. But all he did was go into the front room and then you were there. Were you waiting for him?'

'I stayed up, thinking Minou might call. Instead our guest came in. He was a little surprised to find me there.'

'But then he can't have done anything, can he? Not if you were with him.'

'Ah, but I wasn't all the time. He went back to your room. Perhaps he telephoned. Sent a text.'

'There's no phone in my room and I haven't seen him with a mobile.'

'He has one. He was in my room earlier, talking to me. I had my radio on and it buzzed when he was standing close to it. You know, the way they do when they get interference from a mobile.'

'I've never seen him use it.'

'No.'

'And he's got no one to phone.'

'His sister.'

'You think he's in touch with her?'

'No, not yet.'

I feel like I'm getting my brain rewired. 'Well, who then?!'

'Pent. I reckon Pent might even have slipped him the phone. Maybe told him he would be able to phone his sister, that he could set it up. Maybe. And I bet the price was that he spy on us, let him know if we had any shoes in development. Did you know that SIRP have made copies of every Blake runner we have ever produced? They change the colour, slap on a SIRP logo, market them as SIRP Sprinters and then undercut our prices. It's obvious; SIRP intend to take over. No problem. And he'll get athletes like Ahmet one way or another. He'll be the sponsor. He'll make the rules. He'll try to wipe Blake's out.' He doesn't seem bothered: feet up on the edge of his desk, absently doodling on a pad resting on his lap.

'Do you think he can do it?'

Blake pulls a face. 'Might. I don't know how long we can keep coming up with seriously good new designs, but it wouldn't be the end of the world. Blake's have always come up with something. We didn't make gym shoes when great-grandad was busy rescuing French aristocrats from the guillotine three hundred years ago.' He gives a short laugh. 'The first Blakes were probably a bunch of crooks no better than Pent!'

He swings his feet down. 'Still, I would prefer not to lose this round to him. I want you to win tomorrow, Trokka, throw a bit of mud in SIRP's eye. You're fast. Ahmet said you ran rings around all

Pent's heavies at Heathrow, made them seem as if they were old men. That's what he said. Win your race and give Blake's a plug. You'll be wearing our sponsored kit, remember.' He makes a final flourish on his pad and then closes it. 'We just need to keep a close eye on our friend Ahmet. He's under a lot of pressure. Keep Pent's sticky hands off him. You win, Ahmet wins and that's two blow outs for SIRP. And meanwhile we've just got to hope Minou's tracked down Ahmet's sister. As long as she's out of the frame we have to expect Ahmet to do whatever he thinks is best to get her back, even if that means making a few phone calls to Pent. After all, what does he owe us?'

Blake might be right but I'm not convinced. Not really. I mean this is Ahmet. Someone who's done what he's done – saved his sister from tanks in the middle of a war – isn't going to be packed into Pent's pocket so easily. I just wonder if there's something else going on here that I don't understand. 'You really don't trust him, do you?'

'I don't trust Pent, Trokka. He'll do what he can to get to Ahmet and Ahmet is vulnerable until we find his sister and get her back. I don't blame Ahmet, whatever he does. But if we can, I want to keep him out of Pent's hands. Just remember, Trokka, if

Blake's didn't make money, we couldn't do what we do, what we have done for generations. I know what you're thinking. That we're just rich, that only money is important to us.'

He's wrong. I don't think that at all. They're different, yes. But we're all different. So what. What I say is this: 'I just don't think Ahmet would betray you, us, like that. Doesn't seem the type.'

Blake rubs his eyes. 'Maybe you're right. I don't know, Patroclus. Don't get me wrong, I like Ahmet, but Sir Pent is a spider, you know what I mean? He's got webs all over the place. We've got to be careful, very. That's what I'm saying.'

'OK.' I stand. It's 5 am. Only two hours before I'm going to have to be up again. Weird, I haven't thought about tomorrow's race all day and that's after weeks of thinking about nothing else. And yes, I do want to win, and not just to give Blake runners a plug. And I want Ahmet to win his races and I want us to find his sister. And I wish the Geek was back because she sees things differently to me.

So that's how we leave it. I go back to my bedroom, quietly lay out all my kit for the next day and set the alarm for 7 am so that I have time for a run before breakfast.

Ahmet breathes deeply, sounding a bit like me

when I was pretending for him. Is he a fake? No way of telling.

I have uneasy dreams, running up a hill with huge insects trying to sting me...

Chapter 13

Ahmet seemed genuinely shocked when we told him about the break in at breakfast and he saw the busted window and the shoe gone. I was watching him closely too, just to see if there was a flicker in his expression that would tell me he already knew about it. But I didn't see a hint of anything like that.

He wanted to know if we had called the police. Good question. We hadn't. Blake usually thinks of everything but he had forgotten about the police. I know why. So much double thinking he'd got himself in a twist. Of course he wanted the shoe stolen but he couldn't tell Ahmet in case it got back to Pent.

So there was this whole pantomime put on for the benefit of Ahmet, with Mr Blake telephoning the local police station and the police coming out and wanting to know what had been stolen and whether any of us had heard anything. The policeman pulled a face when we all said we hadn't. More pretending. And in fact they took quite a long time interviewing Mr Blake on his own.

And you know what Mr Blake told us once the police left and we were sitting around the breakfast table in the kitchen? He said that the police were suspicious, thought the whole thing was a fiction! That we had made up the business of the theft and started asking questions about insurance.

Ahmet just drank his orange juice and said nothing. Mrs Blake clucked and kept muttering that the police were so *stupeed*. Blake exchanged looks with his father. 'They think all the break ins are connected to us?'

'Hinted as much.'

'They think we're robbing our own factories?'

'They do.'

'So we can pick up the insurance?'

'Exactly.'

'And why would we want to do that?'

Mr Blake coughed. He'd clearly had enough questions, even from his own son, and retreated behind his newspaper.

'Dad?'

'Sort of thing people do if their business is going down the drain,' he muttered.

'Is our business going down the drain?'

'It will if people think we're just a bunch of spivvy crooks.' He rattled his newspaper crossly and Blake finally stopped his questions.

And that was almost that.

We were all pretty quiet then. Blake turned on the television for the news and there was Pent's face filling the whole screen and his voice purring like a well-fed cat. And what was he talking about? Criminal investigations in the world of athletics and sportswear. Dodgy companies. Corruption. Sponsorship deals. Athletes being smuggled illegally into the country and then being forced to do whatever their sponsors tell them to do. 'It is', purred Pent, 'a most invidious kind of slavery, really, and though I'm not in a position to name names, we all know that Blake's, popular for so long, are now struggling, and I have it under report that they are being investigated for malpractice. I am, of course, desperately sorry that such a reputable company should have any kind of shadow cast over them; but at least we can rely on some ethically sound businesses, such as SIRP, and in today's important races...'

'Turn it off!' snapped Mr Blake, from behind his paper, startling us all, even his wife, who blinked.

'*Cheri*,' she said. '*Doucement*.'

I think even Blake was surprised by his father. 'Dad, don't worry, the man's a liar.'

'Worse! Much worse,' he grumbled, peering over the paper. 'You deal with him, Percy.'

Ahmet looked from father to son, but still said nothing.

'Dad!' There was a note of warning in Blake's voice.

'What? Yes, of course. Bad business. Upsetting, you know. Apologies all round.'

So that was breakfast. Quite a start to the day.

Ahmet and I packed our gear and then Ahmet said goodbye to Mrs Blake. He seemed very serious as he was thanking her for their kindness to him. She seemed a little surprised. I don't know what arrangements had been made but she clearly thought he was due to come back that night. Thinking back on it I wondered if he was actually saying goodbye properly because he didn't expect to see her again.

There was no word from the Geek, which surprised us both, me and Blake, I mean. He texted her, telling her to make contact as soon as she was in the country and that we were expecting to meet up with her at the races in Cambridge. And then we drove south, Mr Blake acting as chauffeur again.

Blake sat in the front with his father, the two of them in deep conversation the whole way, not that Ahmet and I sitting in the back heard anything of what they said because the glass partition was closed.

'Blake business, I expect,' I said to Ahmet.

'Oh yes, I think business is very important to Percy and his father. But this is not for us, I think. We are runners. To run is to face one way, Patroclus. We cannot think of anything other than our goal, our target.'

'The finish line.'

'Yes, but also you must have reason to win and nothing must come between you and this reason. The mind', he said, tapping the side of his forehead, 'and the heart must be clear, pure. Business. Money. This is nothing. You cannot run for these things.'

I didn't tell him our job was to win to give Blake's a plug.

He told me about his home on that journey. It was in a small village up in a mountain valley. He described their house, with its walled yard, cool rooms with narrow slit-windows so they were always shady, the little garden that his grandfather tended, and the stream that roared through the middle of the village in winter but shrank to nothing in the long dry summer.

And he told me about his twin sister. How they had always walked to school together; until times changed and the imam decreed that girls were not allowed to go to school; and how then she would wait for him to come out of class and on the long way home he would tell her everything he had learned. How she ran with him when he ran, and helped with the sheep and the goats when he was herding, and how when she had to do the women's chores in the house he would help, even though this made his father and his brothers angry.

He told me how in his country some girls are married at a young age and the girls' husbands are chosen by the family. And that he and Soroya had made a pact when they were six years old that they would live together always, no matter what their parents said. This was their terrible secret, because in their country children must obey their parents above everything else.

When he was twelve he was sent to a different school, over the mountain in the next valley. A bus would collect him and five other boys and would rattle slowly along the mountain road, sometimes stopping for more boys. Even though the school day was longer and the bus was slow he still gave his sister the lessons he had been taught that day.

When the war came, with its tanks and trucks with grey rockets and bearded fighters, he had been in the next valley at school. The lesson had been torn apart with a terrible explosion that took away the whole of one wall and killed their fierce teacher. All the students remained sitting at their desks, frozen for one or maybe two seconds; and then there was wailing and crying and coughing because of the plaster and smoke but he could see, through the space where the wall had been, great blossoming explosions of orange erupting up the valley, as the tanks rumbled and fired and rolled over mud walls, crumbling houses into dust and dirt.

And he had run.

And there had been nothing in his mind but that he must get to his village before the tanks and the trucks and the bearded fighters moved up over the mountain on the bad road.

He ran through the smoke and shattered houses. There had been shouting and shots but he had closed his mind to everything. He ran and scrabbled straight up the mountain because it was quicker than the road and there was a track he knew.

'My chest was fire, Patroclus,' he said. 'My legs burned. My feet, I had no running shoes, no Blake runners, but I run faster than the tanks and trucks and I come to my village and I cannot call out, there is no air in my lungs. But my father sees me. He sees that my feet are bleeding and he knows I have run and before I can say the word 'tanks' he has called the alarm and everyone is running but my sister is not in the house. She has gone to the place where the bus stops to let us off and though my father tells me to come with him and my other brothers and mother, I do not because I know that today there will be no bus and she will stand there waiting until the tanks come.

'I run through the village and even though the whole of our valley is loud with the thunder of the approaching tanks and lorries, she is still standing, waiting at her place. And she doesn't see me because she is facing down the mountain and she doesn't hear me calling because of all the noise of the motors and the guns beginning to fire again. And maybe some things are destined, because I pulled her away from the road and up into the rocks and we hid there. But the tanks and rockets fired into our village and killed many people even though they were running away. And my family were all killed. And so there is just my sister and I, and this is why she comes here with me, and does not stay in my country.

'But those in our village who lived knew that they were saved because I had brought the warning, the warning I couldn't shout. And when this fighting died away, the imam said I must be a runner, and run for the country. If I run and win, people will take notice. They will say this country is something, not just a place of fighting. So Soroya and I go to Kabul and I do not know how but I am told a big company from England can help a runner like me and this company is Blake's. And they pay for me and Soroya to come here. They make our papers right.' He gives a bitter laugh. 'They say our papers are right but still they take my sister. I think you have war here, Patroclus.'

'What do you mean?'

'There is war against Blake family and this man, Minister Pent, is an enemy, yes?'

I nod. 'Pent is a bad man, Ahmet.'

He shrugs. 'This is not my war.'

'No. But you will run today, won't you? It's important for you, your country.'

'Yes, but remember what I tell you, in the mind of runner there must be nothing that comes between him and his reason for winning.'

I understand what he is telling me. 'Soroya.'

He pulls a face. 'I run for her. And she is not here I know but Percy make me this promise she will come...' He shrugs. 'Who do you run for, Patroclus?'

That takes me by surprise. Who do I run for? I run because I have discovered it is something that I can do. I run for myself. Is that so bad? And I run for my family, although not my sister. I don't tell him that, though.

Chapter 14

Blake was right to be worried about Ahmet at the race. We lost him. Lost him completely.

So much for me keeping an eye. Patroclus the blind, that'll be my new name. Still, no point kicking myself; we've got plenty of enemies only too keen to do that for me.

This is the way it happened.

Cambridge. The junior Internationals. Almost the same set-up as at Tornby but much posher and much bigger: more crowds, more tents and more stands and notice boards. Television crews and officials with armbands, families fussing and coaches talking earnestly. And tension. Excitement wound up tight and ready to snap. Competitors are in their national kit, although most also have a sponsor's logo splashed across their back. There's SIRP yellow everywhere with all the SIRP banners fluttering from tent tops and lining the tracks and stands. There are adverts for other companies too, but suspiciously none for Blake's. When I do see Blake's name it's on one of those big balloons which trails the slogan *'Bin your Blake's and Snatch a SIRP Sprinter.'*

We change into running gear, all three of us, because Blake, although he's still doing his goofy surfer bit for the benefit of Ahmet, decides to have a practice run with us. We ignore the sour looks of two runners in the changing room, both with yellow splashed across their vests, of course.

'Blake's are getting desperate,' one of them says. 'Sponsoring retards now.'

Blake gives his great extra-mega-big braying laugh which freaks them out and they hurry away. 'Spooked by the kook,' says Blake, delighted with himself. Ahmet pretends not to notice. I don't waste time asking Blake what a 'kook' is.

The three of us run a couple of practice laps together. Blake's not bad, too stocky really for a runner, but he's strong. I reckon he could keep going over quite a distance. Ahmet is born to run – long legs that eat up the yards and miles. He lets me match him but keeps the pace just fast enough to make Blake struggle and then, when we have left Blake about fifty metres behind us, Ahmet suddenly stops and steps to the side of the track. I join him.

'There is no friendship in running, Patroclus. When you run, you must run to win,' he says.

'Or because you've no other option,' I say, thinking of his frantic scrambling run up the mountain, the line of tanks like dirty green bugs trundling along the road below. His half-won race for the life of his village, of his family.

We shake hands. He's wrong about friendship, though. There is friendship in running – maybe not in the act of racing, but in this sharing of skill and memories, there is something good.

We turn and watch Blake jogging up to us with an easy, slightly rolling gait. He grins and shakes his head. 'You two can walk faster than I can run,' he says, but I notice that he's not remotely out of breath and I half wonder if he deliberately let the two of us run ahead so we could talk. My race is about to be called; Ahmet has about ten minutes before his.

He has two races this afternoon. The first is the one thousand metres, but his big race is the five thousand. If what all the papers say about him is right, he shouldn't have a problem. Except I know he does. He's going to be thinking about his twin, not the race.

I can't worry about that now, though. I have to do what he says, clear my mind and focus. Mine's the one hundred. Eight competitors. If I'm one of the first three over the line I'll have a good chance of being selected for the junior Olympic team. A long, skinny 'if'. Not what my father says of course. 'You are Greeks, Michael, you will run Olympics, you will win. Greeks, we invent Olympics, of course you win. This is the way it is.'

I see Stick-boy heading for the start line and yes, there are the Bins, Jaco and Stef, pushing people out of the way as if their boy is some spangle-suited wrestler making his way into the ring. I wonder if their brainless wonder, the Maggot, is sleeping off his burglary adventure of last night. With any luck he's still busy picking bits of glass out of his body from the window he smashed.

I take a slow, deep breath. New rules: no more Mr Invisible, not for today; no disappearing; no running away. I stretch up on my toes. I am going to be bigger, faster, stronger. Ahmet seems to have read my mind; he gives me a smile from under his shady eyes and nods.

'Good luck.'

Time to go, so I start to head off, just as Blake's phone beeps a text-alert. 'Minou!' he says. 'Don't wait. I'll fill you in after the race. Go!' He gives us both a wave and the last I see of him is his head bent down, frowning, his two thumbs furiously stabbing at his mobile.

I find myself wishing that Minou was here to see me being visible. But being visible brings trouble, in the shape of Jaco and Stef escorting their albino Stick-boy to the start line.

'Well, if it isn't our old friend, Trokka,' says Jaco when he sees me.

I take a breath and dump one of my oldest rules: never talk back to the Bins. 'Can't Stick-boy find his own way to the start?' I say. 'What a shame. Not much chance of him finding the finish then, is there?'

Jaco looks a bit startled, which makes me feel good, and then he jabs his finger at me. 'Watch your mouth, Trokka. We know where you live, remember.' And then officials hustle him and all the other well-wishers – not that Bins come into that category – off the track.

Stick-boy glares at me under his long white eyelashes. Makes me think of a snake. Are there albino snakes? Should be. He's one. And I wonder why he's running in this race. Pent business. I decide to keep well clear of him.

'This is the runner who tried to trip me in the Nationals,' says the Stick, loudly so that everyone up and down the line can hear.

That makes me laugh.

'Better not try that one here, mate,' says the runner on my left.

'He's lying,' I say.

'Yeah. Right. Just don't try it on me.'

The Stick smirks. I ignore him.

'On your marks.'

I concentrate on the two white lines that stretch into the distance ahead of me: my track, my road, and the way is clear... Focus.

And yes, I won that race. Left Stick-boy standing with nothing but the air in my face. And that finish line – didn't even hear the yelling of the crowds until I was there; heard nothing more than that sea rumble of blood in my ears and the rasp of my breath. Over the line, tape across my chest, and then a quick jump to avoid Jaco who had pushed himself to the front of the crowd pretending he wanted to give me a congratulatory slap on the back. I caught a glimpse of someone behind him, a goofy joker with a giant green frog hat, who I reckon gave our Jaco a brisk shove. Just as well he did, and just as well I still had enough spring in my legs to jump over him and avoid his flailing arms, because I saw the flash of a metal cosh he'd got gripped in his right hand. Some things change but Jaco doesn't. If he'd given me a crack with that thing he could have put me out of the running for a couple of weeks. But he didn't, thanks to Mr Frog.

I just had time to register my win at the officials desk and get back to the track to see Ahmet starting his race. He made it look so easy. He was out in front from the first moment, running easily, but with five, no, six runners trailing him one after the other, all matching strides, like clockwork. Behind them was the rest of the field, shifting and thickening and thinning, but there were no surprise dark horses suddenly accelerating away from the pack to join the leaders.

Slowly the two groups, the first six and the remainder, drew further apart. Lap one. It didn't look as if Ahmet was increasing the pace, nothing visible changed in the swing of his arms or movement of his legs, but the tight line following him began to waver. Number six dropped back a metre and then another. The other front runners all looked as if they had speeded up and yet because Ahmet was comfortably pulling away it was if they were actually slowing down. By the second lap he was twenty paces in the lead.

He was setting a new junior world record and the commentator was working himself into a high-pitched frenzy. The crowd was going wild. I was yelling myself hoarse and jumping up and down like a yo-yo. He could have walked the last ten metres and still won, but he ran like the wind. I half expected him to keep going, through the crowd, over the fences, onto the motorway and disappear somewhere over the horizon heading for Scotland and beyond; but of course he just ended up in a swirl of well-wishers and TV crews and, dressed in a plum-coloured velvet suit, the new Minister for Sport, Sir Pent himself.

I didn't want to stick around. I wanted to find Blake. He must have been watching the race but there was no sign of him. I wondered if Minou's message had been bad news. I also wanted to change, but Blake had said to keep an eye on Ahmet and keep him away from Pent, so I stayed where I was, trying to keep close. I couldn't though. Ahmet was swept up and swallowed by all the racing bigwigs and the last I saw of him before his big race was the back of his head as he was led into the TV commentary box.

'Can't come to harm in there,' said a familiar voice in my ear. 'Too many witnesses.'

I spun round and glimpsed a daft grin under a green frog hat. Blake?

Maybe.

Probably.

But he was immediately swallowed up by the crowd. So I finally went and changed and then made my way to get a good place for the five thousand. I saw the runners coming down to the start line. I saw the plum colour of Pent and a diseased-looking rash of yellow logos from the SIRP crew. I even saw, at least I think I did, the oily smooth dome of the SIRP salesman. I saw nothing of Blake though.

I managed to catch Ahmet's eye. He looked as if he was scanning the stands. I waved. He didn't wave back. His face was a mask. Weird, I thought. He looked defeated, not like someone who had just ripped a fine win and had a strong chance of snatching another.

He didn't though. He ran like a lead chicken. I couldn't believe it when some other runner sloped in ahead of him. And no one tripped Ahmet or pushed him. I saw it all; it was the mirror image of the first race, but back to front exactly. Ahmet was never anywhere but last, right from the gun.

I turned away in disgust.

And that was the last I saw of him.

The drive back was like being in a hearse.

'What happened to him?'

'Pent happened to him,' said Blake.

'I'm sorry. My fault, I was meant to be watching.'

'Not your fault, Trokka, I was watching too and I lost him. I don't even remember him crossing the finishing line.'

That jolted me. Something bad. I suddenly thought of his disappeared sister. 'Do you think he was kidnapped?' I said.

'Pent doesn't need to; he already has a hold over him,' said Blake. 'I saw them together, after his TV interview. I couldn't get to him; too many SIRP thugs in the way. But the two of them were head to head, muttering like a pair of cardinals in a cloister.'

'What!'

Blake grinned. 'One of my father's expressions, just trying it out.' He stared out of the window. 'Pent must have told him something that knocked the stuffing right out of him. Tell me, Trokka, what did you two talk about when you were running together before the races?'

So, I had been right. He had wanted us to talk – probably felt that Ahmet would be more likely to confide in another runner than in him. Maybe I was beginning to understand Blake the Pimpernel after all. I told him that Ahmet was worried about his sister, and that he was pinning his hopes on us rescuing her.

'Nothing about Pent?'

'No.'

Then he told me what Minou had texted him. 'Calais. That's where Ahmet's sister is, so he won't have to worry much longer. We'll have her back in a jiffy.'

'And what about Minou? I thought she was supposed to be back here.'

'She was. Change of plan. She hasn't yet found where in Calais Ahmet's sister is being held. She's going to nose around and then come back.'

So much for the old 'back in a jiffy' bit.

Blake pulled a face. 'Hope she doesn't have trouble getting back into the country.'

'What? Minou? Why? She's got a UK passport.'

'Yes, well, Pent's empire seems to have stretched from sport to immigration. If we don't make a move soon, he'll become prime minister.'

'You're not serious!' I don't know much about politics. Well, I don't know anything is closer to the truth, except that Mum and Dad vote and Dad always complains that he doesn't like anyone he votes for. But he would never vote for Pent, not in a million years. 'No one would vote for him,' I said.

'I don't think something like that would stop him. Except we're not going to let it happen. We're going to get him, Trokka. We're going to have so much evidence that they'll have to lock him up for good. Our next move, though, is to get Soroya back. And to do that I need to have a look at a map.'

'Map?'

'Calais.'

'Don't you know where it is?' My geography isn't brilliant but even I know where Calais is.

'I want to see what's near it, Trokka, and why Minou's trail ended there. There has to be a reason. Entry and exit. Somewhere people are on the move. A good place to hide someone, maybe.'

It was only when I was getting out of the car outside the café that Blake mentioned my race. He leaned over and shook my hand. 'Well done, Trokka. You ran a brilliant race. I should have said it before. I owe you a new pair of Blake's. And the way I'm thinking we may have some hard running ahead of us. Keep your screen on; I'll make contact later tonight.'

And then he was gone. I pushed open the door to the café and was greeted by the sound of my mother and father, and extraordinarily my sister too, shouting and singing and waving tea towels at me. It was terrible. You know what it was? Queen. 'We are the Champions' changed of course to 'He is the Champion'.

After all the hugging and crying and cheek pinching I managed to ask, 'How did you know I won the race?'

'Your friend, that nice boy, Percy,' says my mother. 'He telephoned us.'

'Poor him with his sticky-out ears, you know,' says my father. 'But good boy. You bring his mother and father to our restaurant, Michael.'

'Yes, Dad.'

As soon as I could, I slipped up to my room. Champion. I didn't like to tell them that we had lost our champion.

I turned on the computer. Instant Messenger told me I'd a new message. I clicked on it. There was one word: POINTPERDU.

Chapter 15

Pointperdu?

I google it, and slowly the penny drops.

Of course. The camp. Where the French have been holding migrants who've been trying to get into Britain but don't have the papers. Illegals who've tramped and trucked and struggled halfway round the world.

The perfect place to hide Soroya. Pent wanted her out of the country, but close enough to be able to use her to keep the world's number one junior runner under his thumb. Sick. And what's worse is that for the moment, until we know exactly where she is, we can do nothing except wait for the Geek's return.

There's two long days with no word from anyone: not the Geek, nor Blake, nor Ahmet, but that's no surprise. The only words I hear are: 'Michael, do this for me.' My parents suddenly seem to find a million and one things for me to do in the kitchen. Then, at about six o'clock on the second day, when I've just escaped up to my room, my mobile vibrates: text message.

I'm coming round now.

She's back!

Ten minutes later there's the sound of feet on the stairs and a knock at the door.

'Hello, Patroclus,' she says, in her usual matter-of-fact way, as she comes into the room. 'You managed to make Sir Pent look silly on television. That was clever of you.'

That seems like a long time ago now, and a small victory after everything else that's happened.

'Thanks.'

She's in one of those moods where she won't just come out and tell me what I want to know but has to stalk about my room, picking up everything and putting it down in a different place.

'Have you spoken to Blake?'

'Not yet. And you won your race, too. Your father told me that.' She grimaces. 'Patroclus, he told me three times! You'll have to get him to calm down a bit. He's so...'

'Greek?'

'Why are you such a daddy's boy, Patroclus?'

I think she's a bit spiky about family things because she never mentions her own father. I mean, I know she likes my parents but she still has a go at me from time to time. I ignore it. 'So you don't know about Ahmet, then?'

That surprises her. 'What about him?'

I tell her how he disappeared after his race.

'And you were meant to be looking after him. Bit careless, Patroclus...'

'Blake was there, too!'

'I was only joking.'

I'm not sure I'll ever be able to recognise when the Geek is joking; she always sounds like she's just stating facts. 'Are you going to tell me about your trip to France, or are you just going to rearrange everything in my room?' I say. 'Can you put that back?' She has my plastic model of the minotaur and is pulling a face at it as if it's the most stupid thing she's ever seen. She doesn't know any of the Greek stories.

'All right. Don't be so grumpy, Patroclus. It's bad luck Ahmet has gone, especially since I found out where his sister is.'

'You found her! In the camp? Did you talk to her?'

'Yes, I saw her. I'm pretty sure it was her but no, I couldn't talk to her.'

Eventually she fills me in with the details of her trip. I am seriously impressed with how she managed everything: catching a train to Paris, making contact with names given to her by Blake, tracking Soroya across the city and all the way to Calais...

'Catching a train isn't very hard, Patroclus.'

'And speaking French?'

'I know French. It's my mother's first language. She's from Senegal.'

'I knew that; I just didn't know you spoke French.'

'I never told you, that's why.' She smiles. 'Do I make you cross, Patroclus?' She sits on the edge of my bed.

'No, you're just weird, but you can't help it.'

'I see.'

She tells me she spent a whole day hunting around Calais but the trail had gone cold. She even wondered if Soroya had already been smuggled back into the UK – except that didn't make sense after all the effort Pent had gone to in having her deported. It was Blake who had put two and two together and come up with Pointperdu.

Blake had also told her not to go into the camp, that it would be too dangerous and she'd end up trapped there. I wondered about that, and actually reckoned they would find her so sharp-tongued they would drive her to the Channel Tunnel and put her on the first train home.

She had ignored Blake's 'advice'.

'But it was an order!'

'It was advice,' she says flatly. 'It's not that hard to get in there. They've got guards. Armed police. Boots, guns, jackets with loads of pockets. The sort of things boys like. They looked quite fierce but they don't seem to do very much. There's wire all round the camp but people come and go. I just tagged onto a family going in and nobody asked me anything. There are so many people in there they can't be bothered to check papers. Anyhow, most of them probably don't have papers because that's why they're in there.'

According to the Geek it was more a maze than a camp, and almost as big as a town. There were warehouses partitioned up into cells and rooms, and those box-like containers they load on trucks and ships, masses of them, emptied out and made into temporary living quarters. And tents, too. She had to be careful. Everyone was suspicious, chasing her on if she stood too long near anyone's living area. She gave up trying to ask questions because it was dizzy-making: hardly anyone spoke French or English, just bits and scraps muddled in with whatever was their home language, and anyway, they didn't want to talk.

She ended up walking round and round, down twisty alleys and corridors, and everywhere there were men standing around in ones and twos, bored, playing cards, arguing. Then she passed a container that had two men standing at the doorway, only they weren't talking to each other, but leaning up against the hot metal sides, eyeing everyone who went by. They looked like they were guarding the place, and they wore better clothes than most people there. One of them had a gold watch. She hurried past, pretending not to look at them. The door was shut of course, but after she had passed by she doubled back. If someone was inside there had to be an air vent or window or something – all the others she'd seen had been adapted in some way to make them habitable.

And she was right, there was a window, but covered in mesh. She hoisted herself up, peered in and saw a girl, or young woman, sitting at a table, listening to a radio playing Arabic music. It had to be

Soroya. She was sure. She was about to call out but at that moment one of the guards decided to wander down the alleyway and saw her. She ran.

'I was like a rat,' she says proudly. 'Very fast, Patroclus.'

'You ran!' She always makes a thing about not running anywhere.

'Don't be silly, Patroclus. I was being chased, of course I ran.'

She ran and lost the man chasing her by slithering under a container that had been raised up on blocks. She saw his tan shoes walking by and then coming back again. He didn't check underneath. Probably just thought she was a petty thief and gave up. She stayed there, though, until it began to get dark. Then it was curfew, 9 pm, and that meant the gates would be closed. Her only choice was to find somewhere to kip down for the night and slip out in the morning; find a break in the wire, or somewhere she could climb over. Climbing is the Geek's speciality.

She didn't have to, though. She said there were so many groups huddling up to the fence, waiting to break through, it was practically like rush hour. She tagged onto a group of boys who cut a small hole in the wire and didn't seem to mind her following them. They crawled for twenty yards and then dipped down into a ditch. Then they scuttled off towards the entrance of the Channel Tunnel. She felt sorry for them because they didn't have a chance of getting through – she'd already checked the security, thinking maybe that would be the way Blake would want to get Soroya back into Britain. There were huge fences, and lights and patrols and dogs. 'They can even detect animals: bats, foxes. Nothing gets past, unless it's legal.'

It was different for her: a twenty-minute hike west to the little town of Pointperdu. She picked up a taxi to Calais and then bought a ticket for the next ferry. An immigration officer at Dover tried to find something wrong with her passport but he was just being difficult. He had to let her through eventually. Easy really.

'And you're sure it was her, Ahmet's sister? Did you see what she was like, or what she was wearing?'

She thinks for a minute. 'Jeans, blue, red top, short-sleeved, something gold on her wrist, and something round her neck. Odd shape, gold or brass, a bit like the top of a pen. She was wearing a scarf on her head.'

If only Ahmet was here. He'd probably know what to ask. If he was here, he would probably believe in us more, believe that we weren't just a bunch of kids, but could get his sister back. But he's not, and we haven't got her back yet.

'Do you think we can?'

'Get her out?'

I nod.

'I don't know. That's Blake's speciality, thinking up cunning plans. I'm tired, Patroclus. Do you think I can stay here tonight?'

'Of course.' I get a sleeping bag and an air mattress out while she rings Blake. I pick up the second phone and the three of us try to figure out a plan of action. But at the moment it seems as if Pent has all the cards. And the junior Olympics are in less than three days. Seventy-two hours. And if Ahmet doesn't run, who are the runners most likely to win the gold?

Blake and I run through the other competitors in Ahmet's race, the big one, the five thousand metres. France? No. Germany, maybe, they've got a strong team. Spain, possibly... We go through them all. All good, none clear favourites. The only frontrunner is Ahmet.

The Geek yawns. She's doodling on my pad, bored. She's got no interest in any sport, really, other than climbing. 'What about us?' she says absently.

'Hm?'

'Us. Aren't you running, Patroclus? You won that last race, didn't you, so you'll be in the British team.'

'Don't be silly. I don't run the five thousand.'

'Why not?'

'I'm a sprinter, that's why. And you've got to be selected to be in the team and I haven't been selected – not yet, anyway.'

'It's not much further. Just a few zeroes.'

'What about the albino?' says Blake suddenly.

'Stick-boy? Not much of a sprinter, more of a distance runner, I reckon.'

'Don't seem to have anything for the one hundred but I've got the Brit team for the five thousand up here on the screen: Scillock and two others, West and Barns. Never heard of them, but that's him, isn't it? Scillock, the Stick.'

'Scillock. Yes. He's a Pent runner. Has Jaco and the Bins nannying him around all the time.'

'I noticed him,' says Blake. 'He just scraped in fourth at the Internationals, but the reason I clocked him was that he didn't seem to be making any effort at all; wasn't even slightly puffed. Someone on the committee likes him, that's for sure, because he's in.'

'Pent,' I say. 'Pent chairs the committee. I bet he's wheeled and dealed to get his athletes selected for the big races. I bet the other two are SIRP runners, too.'

'And if anyone he sponsors picks up gold, SIRP will be a world corporation. And Blake's will be history.'

'What! You sponsor other runners, don't you? What about the other events?'

'Six, not counting Ahmet or you, and, listen to this, Dad's just told me that all six of them have all rolled over to Pent, signed up with SIRP. He must have made them some totally giant offer.'

'I wonder what's happened to them...'

'Forget them, Trokka; it's Ahmet we have to find.'

'You didn't get any more information from your spy camera in the shoe?'

The Geek rolls her eyes but she doesn't interrupt. I know what she's thinking though: leave those two alone for one minute and it's all gadgets and stupid boys stuff. She's wrong though – Blake's gadgets are the real business.

'No, just some people we've yet to identify. Scientists working for Pent most likely. Now, listen, we've three days. Only three days. So, what's our priority? Find Ahmet or bring back his sister?'

'Soroya,' says the Geek, without hesitation.

'Both,' I say. 'They're both a priority. We can't

choose one over the other. Ahmet has to run. But he won't run, one, unless we find him and two, unless Soroya is there to see him run. No choice.'

'Well,' says the Geek, looking at me with some surprise, 'Patroclus has spoken.'

There's silence at the end of the line. Then Blake says, 'Thanks, Trokka. You're right, there's no choice. Win or lose, our mission is to get the two together in time for the race.'

'So that Ahmet can get the gold he deserves.'

'And Britain can lose. Not very patriotic, are we?'

'The Pimpernel isn't anything to do with patriotism,' says Blake, 'just doing what's right.'

And so that's it. Nothing decided yet, but Blake says we're to meet up early tomorrow and he'll have a plan of action for us. I'm only too happy to leave him to do the thinking – my brain feels like a tomato sliced up, slurped with oil and then left in the sun for three days... It is not good to think like this.

The Geek curls up and goes to sleep almost immediately while I lie in bed and think about what she did and whether I would ever be brave enough to do anything like that. All I do is run, run in big circles. That's what racing is. It doesn't seem much, does it?

Chapter 16

The cream envelope sits propped against the bowl of fruit my mother always puts out for breakfast. My father has a chunk of bread with honey and yoghurt, and complains about the honey. 'This English bees are starving all the time, Michael. What is it they are eating? Nothing. Always raining so they don't go out. Greek bees like pine tree, mimosa. They like Greek things...' Well, that's him. My sister says everything makes her sick before twelve o'clock, but I think she mainly means us. Me, I like cereal. I like toast. I like orange juice. That's as close to fruit as I get. 'You will all lose your teeth and your hair will fall out,' complains my mother. 'You will be sick and turn yellow.' My father checks his hair and his moustache in the mirror and then tells her he loves her very much.

This happens most days. Today, there is the letter.

'What is it, Michael? You do not have tax. Is this government?' He is getting excited.

'He is too young for army. Is it army, Michael?'

I haven't opened it yet.

'He is too young for army, Anna...'

My mother flaps her hand at him as if he's one of those Greek bees he keeps going on about. 'Let him open it. Michael, open it and stop your father fussing.' She is much more concerned about feeding the Geek, who to my mother's delight is helping herself to fruit. She has eaten a peach and taken a fig and now my mother is darting backwards and forwards fetching her grapes, a little bit of melon, and some cherries. 'Turkish,' she whispers so my father doesn't hear, 'but very good.'

I open the envelope. Inside is a thick card with embossed silver lettering. It looks so fancy it might have come from Buckingham Palace.

'What is it, Patroclus?'

'I'm on the team.'

There it is:

Michael Patroclus, you have been selected to represent Her gracious Majesty and the British people at the junior Olympics in the One Hundred Metres race.

'Of course,' roars my father, 'I know this! We shall win, Michael. We shall soar with wings like Icarus!' And he gives me a squashing hug.

Everyone is happy, and even Clara mumbles something that doesn't have 'Leave me alone!' in it.

At the stop waiting for the bus to take us out to Blake's, Minou says, 'You only read out part of the card, Patroclus. Why's that?'

Nothing gets past the Geek.

'I have to present myself tomorrow at the SIRP Academy outside Cambridge for a presentation and briefing.'

'Briefing by who?'

'Sir Maximus Pent, Minister for Sport.'

That was surprise number one. Surprise number two is what we see when we arrive at the Blake house. Their electric gate looks as if a herd of wild buffalo has smashed through it. Since there aren't too many buffalo in this part of the world, the real answer isn't hard to find. One of those massive four-wheel drive cars is sticking out of the front door of the house. It looks like the house is chewing on a scromped-up metal cigar. The door has disappeared, great chunks of brickwork have been knocked out of the frame and there's glass everywhere. The curtains are closed upstairs.

'Wow! What do you think happened?' I ask the Geek. 'Drunk joy riders, what...'

'Patroclus! This was a ram raid.' She takes a picture.

But I'm already running full-tilt round to the kitchen door. Blake's there. He says he's been up all night, and we can see he's buzzing like a bluebottle. His parents have gone back to bed. They've had the police round but they can't get the smashed car taken away until they've had it checked for prints. The police kept asking whether the Blakes thought it might be someone from the factory, someone with a grudge.

'It's not, of course. It's our SIRP friends again. I knew they'd be back because they only got the shoe last time, not the plans. Brilliant, except I wish they hadn't axed the house. Terror tactics, Trokka.' He rubs his hands as if 'terror tactics' is exactly what every Blake particularly relishes. Then he pulls me into the house. 'Come in, Trokka. Have coffee, scrambled eggs, toast, whatever you want. Minou with you? Great. Give me five minutes. I need a shower.'

He probably needs to be unplugged from the mains circuit but I don't think that'll happen. Minou and I get ourselves a drink and switch on the radio to catch the local news, but there's no mention of the break in.

When Blake comes back he's still running on overdrive, but at least he looks normal: face scrubbed, bleached hair brushed back and wearing jeans and a check shirt with the sleeves rolled up. He looks much older for some reason – he could pass for sixteen or seventeen. It's funny, I feel a bit dwarfed by him, which I've never felt before.

As he bustles around making breakfast he takes us through the whole ram raid incident. How he and his parents thought someone had thrown a bomb into the sitting room, how the downstairs had been filled with smoke and that when he'd run down, he'd seen a couple of figures running out from the work room and pelting across the gravel. 'Masked,' he says. 'One of them was Stef, though.' His blue eyes are glinting with amusement at the memory.

'How do you know, if they were masked?'

'Took a guess. He was running like a goof anyway, so I called out to him, "Hey, Stef, you left the main envelope behind." He actually stopped and said, "What?" Can you believe it? Whoever was with him just grabbed him and hauled him out.'

'And they had a van waiting again.'

'Same one.'

Sammy holda, I think to myself. 'And so they didn't get the plans?'

'No, of course they did. I had TOP SECRET PLANS stamped in huge letters on the folder and it was the only thing on the desk, with a light shining down on it! Not even a baboon could have missed it. I've been expecting them back every night. Each time they've raided a factory they've gone for the plans. All SIRP can do is copy, that's why they have to have diagrams and stuff, like one of those self-assembly manuals. I bet you their team will be wearing our Trojan runners on the big day.'

He shovels up the last of his scrambled egg and butters his third bit of toast. 'They took another shoe I've been working on, too.'

'You didn't tell us,' I say.

'No. It didn't work quite how I hoped. It was a distance shoe. I was thinking of you, Trokka.'

'I do sprints.' Patroclus the dasher.

'Yes, well, you never know...distance might be handy. Anyhow it's gone and they're welcome to it.' He pushes away his plate.

Minou's been watching him intently. I think she's impressed by his huge appetite. 'They've really got it in for your family, haven't they?' she says.

'Oh yes. Forces of darkness closing in and all that sort of thing. Funny how they don't know it's not my family that's the enemy.' He looks at us both. 'But us, the Pimpernel.'

The Geek nudges me and I give him my SIRP invitation.

He stares at it like I've just slipped him the Holy Grail. Then he puffs out his cheeks. 'Outstanding!' he says quietly. 'Well done, Trokka.' Then he suddenly leaps to his feet, spreads his arms wide in the air and shouts, 'I don't believe it! What a gift!' And, putting on a mad American preacher's voice, he roars, 'Oh, Mr Pent! How you will repent!'

His mother appears at the door, shakes her head and disappears back up the stairs.

'It could be a trap,' says Minou. 'What if they just want Patroclus to disappear because they have another runner they want to replace him with?'

The thought had occurred to me but I hadn't said anything because I want to run – I really do.

'A trap,' says Blake, 'of course it's a trap. This is Pent, he can't help but set traps. He is the spider, but we're going to outspider the spider because they won't expect Trokka to have any backup; and you and me, Minou, are backup.' He sits back down and snatches another bite of toast. 'I just knew we had to get into the SIRP Academy,' he says between munches. 'It's obvious when you think about it. Where else is Ahmet going to be?'

I try not to pull a face. I should have thought of it, but didn't.

'And this, my clubbies,' he says, waving the invitation, 'is the perfect way in.' He holds up a hand to stop us asking questions. 'Where else? Trokka will go there to shoot the curl.'

We look blank.

'Come on guys – the presentation! Trokka surfs in there and then hangs ten on the back of his board. Easy McSneezy.' He jumps up again. 'And now, my little grommies, just a few things to show you,' and he hurries out of the kitchen.

'You mean Patroclus needs us as a safety net in case he falls down again,' the Geek mutters. She's nosing around the kitchen, picking up bits and pieces and putting them back again. Then she starts leafing through a stack of pages on the sideboard – it looks like a computer print-out.

'I'm not going to fall again,' I say. 'And put that back, Minou. It could belong to his parents.'

'I don't think so.' She sniffs. 'And what you really mean is,' she turns a page, 'you won't get worked. Or drilled. Or, here it is now, totally axed! Ha!'

'What *is* that?'

'Surfing glossary!'

'You're kidding!'

And we both laugh because, great as he is, Blake is such a fake!

Still, we have to hand it to him, he was certainly mega-busy last night. Having made up his mind that the SIRP Academy was where Ahmet was holed up, he had spent what was left of the night preparing outfits and disguises for us to use in our attempt to get him out. He had SIRP uniforms, tracksuits and even what looked like a flying suit with goggles and a helmet. Amazing.

'We're on the lookout for a chopper, chaps,' he says.

'A chopper?' I shake my head; he's more cracked than a Greek statue. I'm about to point out that none of us knows how to fly a kite, let alone a helicopter, but Minou nudges me to shut up. Blake's reeling off the outline of his plan.

'We find Ahmet. We find out what Pent's plans are for athletes like him. We get Ahmet out of the SIRP Academy. We give him a pair of these.' He holds up a model of Blake runners that I've not seen before. 'Behold the very latest design. Made exactly for his feet. Measured him up as soon as he arrived.

Is he going to like them or what?'

They look like they've stepped out of a dream. They're ghost-white with tiny threads of pale green running up from the sole like veins. The soles are deeper than in the standard runner and made not from rubber but from a kind of gel. 'Wicked,' I say.

'They are, aren't they.' He grins. 'I've got a pair for you, too.'

Wow!

'Well, of course, you're a Blake's athlete, Trokka. Wake up!' Then he's back in planning mode. 'OK. We give him these then tell him we're off to get his sister. That should pump him a bit. Then we ride the sky to Calais for mission number two. The details of which', he says, patting a second folder he has lying on the table, 'are in here. Stoked!'

I hand Blake his surfing glossary. He doesn't even blink. 'Oh, I just printed that out for you two, my little clubbies, so you'd understand what I'm saying.'

Chapter 17

When I finally see Ahmet sitting on an old cane chair and staring out of the window, one of my father's odd sayings comes into my head and won't go away: 'Icarus will not fly today'.

I always liked the story of Icarus and his father, who made themselves wings from feathers and wax but ended up flying too close to the sun. Meltdown. Dad says the Icarus thing when he has to cancel a plan, and since he always has about a million plans, he says it a lot.

Four days, that's how long he's been here, and he's changed somehow. He's a fallen Icarus now. Worn out, slumped in the chair, some worn SIRP baseball cap on his head, the peak carelessly twisted sideways; his expression blank as a prison wall.

'Ahmet!'

He looks up, startled, and then frowns. 'Michael! Why do you come to this place?'

Not such a great welcome then.

A silver airstream coach had picked up all invitees from outside Cambridge station and a slick SIRP rep smooth-talked us all the way to the gleaming SIRP headquarters. There were about twenty of us on the coach, all about my age, all hopeful, all excited; all loving the party bags on each seat packed with wrist bands, caps, cotton shirts (all tagged with the SIRP logo), loving the movie that showed the SIRP Academy as some sixteen-star luxury resort, loving the sweet 'energy' drink that came in a space-age silver bottle.

I didn't like any of it. Maybe I'm just suspicious of gifts, especially since I know Sir Pent is about as generous as a hungry anaconda. I might have been imagining things but I could swear that those twenty very boisterous, energy-spinning individuals who boarded the bus at Cambridge were strangely quiet and unquestioning by the time we pulled into the long drive that led up to the Academy.

I didn't touch the 'energy' drink but I admit I was pretty awestruck when I saw the place, the Pentdemonium.

The white-stone drive cut between green lawns, with marked out tracks. The white on green looked so crisp it seemed practically edible. And the building itself was all glass and gleaming stainless steel. There wasn't a front door but an arched entrance – it was like being drawn into a fairy story, Cinderella's glass slipper turned into a glass palace.

We queued. We registered. We were tagged and labelled. An official in SIRP yellow told us we had a strict schedule. There would be a tour followed by a welcome ceremony where the Minister for Sport would address all the young athletes. But what did Pent want from us? I put up my hand.

'Yes.'

'Is SIRP intending to sponsor everyone here?' I asked.

'Oh no.' The reply came back as slick as top-grade olive oil. 'There will be a selection process just after the tour.'

I looked around me to see if anyone was going to ask about this. No one did. They all nodded and smiled. Drugged or bewitched, or maybe a bit of both.

'Thank you,' I said. I had no intention of getting myself singled out as a troublemaker; though if Blake and Minou were right and this was a trap, I wondered how long I had before I found myself being zapped down a waste chute to the dungeons. Even fairy palaces have dungeons.

The tour started. I knew we would only be shown the shiny surfaces. The building was big enough to hide a hundred Ahmets and I wasn't going to waste time seeing places where Ahmet wasn't. When I discovered that the tour would only be taking in the ground floor, I drifted back to the tail of the procession, and as soon as we passed an elevator, I ducked back. Held my breath and pressed for the lift to come.

The doors slipped open and, hoping that my luck would hold, I stepped in. Empty. Yes! I stripped off my top and shovelled myself into the SIRP kit that Blake had put together for me: yellow T-shirt and shiny yellow tracksuit bottoms with a white coat on top. Grim, I know. Minou had wanted to take a picture when I tried it on, but I wouldn't let her.

I pulled out the clipboard and bundled up the clothes I'd come in, ready to stuff them into the first bin I came across. Blake had insisted on the clipboard. 'Always works,' he said. 'Makes you look official. No one questions someone with a clipboard.' I thought he was being a bit optimistic, but here I was with the clipboard tucked up under my arm.

First floor. This was where I reckoned it would get interesting.

It did.

The corridor had no deep-pile carpet; the walls were dispiriting hospital-green, the air was cool and tanged with a sharp smell of sweat. I was near a gym. I had to be. I headed for the double doors at the far end of the corridor but just as I was about to push through, two SIRP personnel almost crashed into me coming from the opposite direction. A man and a woman, white coats over their yellow gear, and both carrying clipboards!

'Sorry!'

'Sorry!'

They barely gave me a glance, though I heard the woman saying: 'Did you see? Bit young for the job, wasn't he?'

But the door swung shut behind me before I could catch the reply. I was about to burst into a headlong sprint but they didn't come charging after me, and anyway I was in a closed-off room, one side of which was a wide smoky window. And there, on the other side of the glass, was the gym.

Knowing Pent, I was expecting the gym from hell, but in fact it looked uber-tech: rows of gleaming treadmills, and flat screens on all the walls with 3D digital line-images of each person pounding away. The people themselves, who had wires taped to their bodies, didn't look so good though; sweat gleamed on their faces, arms and legs, and their vests were dripping wet. They looked beyond exhaustion. But they didn't stop, didn't climb off, didn't get a drink, just kept pounding on to the rhythm of the loud music which filled the room. I wondered what kind of promises Pent must have made to them. Poor suckers.

An assistant or guard – it was hard to tell which – stood by each machine, clipboard in hand, making notes every few seconds. At the far end of the gym was a long desk, banked with computer screens. Two boffin-looking assistants sat there, their fingers dancing like scuttling spiders on the keyboards. Behind them were two floor-to-ceiling screens; the one on the right had a rotating line-image of a running shoe, the design of which seemed to be shifting slightly all the time; the one on the left flicked through each of the people working out in the gym. Each piece of film lasted about ten seconds and then was replaced by yet another digital line-image surrounded by red flashing arrows labelled *stress point* and *bone erosion* and *muscle waste*. Numbers flickered and changed constantly beside them.

I couldn't move. It was hypnotic, like being in an aquarium, except with none of that relaxing green light. This was harsh and stark and the music and machines thundered like a migraine, so strongly that even in my viewing room, I could feel the juddering of all those feet hitting the rubber treads.

It made me think of rats and mice in one of those scientific laboratories...but what were they being tested for? The ultimate shoe? Or maybe what makes the perfect running body? Whatever it was, it was pure Pent. He didn't care what happened to these young athletes so long as he got his research.

A red light flashed on and started to pulse. The music cut out. A buzzer made an urgent 'I'm about to explode' noise and the machines slowed and stopped; the runners hung for a moment like rag dolls on their treadmills and then, one after the other they unplugged themselves and, with unsteady legs, stepped down. One of them keeled over and had to be carried out by assistants. With heads bowed and chests heaving they left the gym through the door at the far end from all the computer consoles. Then another group filed in and one by one took their places on the vacated machines. No sign of Ahmet.

He had to be here somewhere, though, I was sure of it. I checked the time. I'd been five minutes. How long before they missed me? I hurried out of the viewing room and strode, as if I was on urgent business, along the corridor. What would I find next? Changing rooms? Rest area? Cells? Would the athletes get any kind of medical check, I wondered?

I rounded a corner and instantly knew that I had found what I was looking for because there was a sign which said: STRICTLY NO ENTRY.

A bulky man in yellow and black, a bit like an oversized wasp, stood guard in front of the door; his head a grizzled dome of black stubble and a stubby silver cosh hanging from his bulging waistline.

He looked at me suspiciously. I tried not to look at the cosh but I saw the red button on it. Electric. More cattle prod than cosh. If he jabbed anyone with that, it would deliver a shock that would bang them halfway into next week.

'Routine check,' I said, making to pass him and go into the room.

'I see.' He stayed where he was, blocking my way. 'I've had no notification. Can't let anyone in here without notification. Strictly no admittance.' Pause. I could almost hear the brain cogs ticking round. 'Bit young for this, aren't you?'

'It's Farsi I have to find,' I said, ignoring his comment about my age, deciding that my best bet was distraction. 'We need to take more exact measurements of his feet. Did you know he used to run barefoot?' I reckoned a basic appeal to prejudice might do the trick. 'Ridiculous what some foreigners do, eh?'

The guard shifted slightly and I noticed his hand drop away from the cosh. 'Ignorance, if you ask me,' he said. 'He's not in this shift. Be down in the rest area. Know where that is?'

'Course.' I gave him a friendly nod and carried on past. Well, it was fifty-fifty that it would be that way. But to say I didn't know would have been a real giveaway, even to a gorilla like him.

I felt the hairs on the back of my neck prickle as I marched on. Any second, Patroclus, I told myself, get ready to sprint like you've never sprinted before. But there was no shout, no call, no sound of running feet after me. I pushed through yet another set of doors. My lucky day. It couldn't have been easier. There, up on the wall: 'Rest Area'. I was nearly home and dry.

I found myself in a big, dimly lit lounge. Televisions flickered along the walls. Young, tired and mostly very thin-looking boys and girls sat facing the screens. Two were playing a silent game of table tennis. More than half of them seemed to be asleep, eyes closed, jaws open. And not one of them was Ahmet.

'Ahmet Farsi?' I said to one of the table tennis players.

'What?'

'Ahmet Farsi? He's from Afghanistan. Have you seen him?'

'In the Panorama Lounge,' said the washed-out girl at the other end of the table, waiting to serve. 'He don't like the TVs. Down the end.'

'Thanks.' I looked around. It was more like a young offenders centre than a training academy. 'Can't you leave?' She looked blank. 'Don't you want to get out of here?'

'We're training,' said the boy. 'No pain, no gain. Come on, Seffie.'

'Don't you want to go home?' I said to the girl.

She shrugged and served the ball.

Ping. Pong. Ping. Pong.

That, and the murmur of the TVs turned down low was the only sound in the room. No one even looked up as I hurried through. Too worn out to think.

Pent could get an Olympic gold for lying.

The Panorama Lounge was a wide, curved room with a massive window looking out onto the grounds. There was only one person in there. He seemed small, dwarfed by the size of the room, the wide expanse of glass and the blue sky beyond it.

Ahmet.

Chapter 18

'Michael! Why do you come to this place?'

He looks at me at first with surprise and then his eyes narrow with disgust. 'You work for them!' It's the outfit. I told you, it looks grim.

'No, I don't. I've come to get you.'

'Why?'

'Ahmet!'

Any second the alarm is going to go. It has to. I think about ice so thin it would crack under the weight of a gnat – that's how thin. Yes, I'm agitated, but I'm trying not to show it.

'What?'

'Ahmet, what are you doing here? Is this how SIRP is helping you prepare for the big race? You look wrecked.'

'I've been on the treads.'

'Like those other suckers in there! You want to be like them. What did he promise you, Ahmet? What was the magic deal?'

'He promises Soroya will come,' he says, turning back to the window. 'He promises he can bring her to me. He is minister; he can do this. Blake is boy. You are boy. And this Pimpernel, he is boy-joke, boy-game. So I wait here.' He's flatter than a pancake.

'But he's a liar! You know he's a liar!'

He shrugs. Maybe he thinks we're all liars. This makes me cross. 'Don't you want to run?' I snap. This is a different me altogether. 'We have twenty-four hours to the race. Twenty-four. That's all. Why do you think Pent has you here? Because he doesn't want you to run. Why doesn't he?'

'Because...'

I'm not looking for answers from him. I want him up and moving.

'Because you'll win if you run. Because he has someone he thinks will get the gold, but only if you're not there. He's conned you! And now you don't know how to recognise who your friends are. You know who's got your sister? He has. Got her locked up in Pointperdu. And you know who's getting her out? We are! You're an idiot, Ahmet!'

His head jerks back, like I've given him a slap. For

an instant he even looks angry. Good. I'm angry. I usually think too much to get angry but I'm angry now. I want to shake him. If I could run like him, I'd never stop; I'd be running so fast I'd take off from the edge of the world and fly: Icarus.

'You say you know where Soroya is. You see her?' He points at me. 'You, Michael, you see her?'

'Minou found her. I can tell you what she was wearing though – jeans, gold bracelet, red top. Head scarf, right?'

He's looking at me now, taking me seriously. He nods. 'Yes, this is how she is. Was there nothing else?'

'Yes. Some kind of pendant round her neck. Minou said it was maybe gold, like a pen top.'

'OK. OK, Michael. You know what this is that you describe: a case of a bullet; one of many we find in the village. Soroya takes some earth from the village and she keep it there. In Kabul we make it in a necklace. It is what we have of our home.' He gets up. 'I make mistake. I come with you but they say I am guest and I do not think they will want me to leave.'

That's what I think, too.

It's time to move fast. Time to show him we're professionals. 'This isn't Blake and me, Ahmet. This is a Pimpernel operation.'

'Yes?' He looks back at me. 'Is he with you, this Pimpernel?'

'No. Not yet. You'll meet him soon enough. First, get you outside. Second, airlift out of here and third, we go for Soroya. Blake said to give you these. For the race.'

And that was Blake's plan! 'Don't worry about the details,' he said. 'We'll use Pent's helicopter and bail out of here when they start all their speeches. Wing and a prayer, Trokka. We'll snatch Soroya from Pointperdu and be back in time for the race. Just have a little faith,' he said. A little! A couple of truck-loads would be handy.

Ahmet holds the shoes in his hands without looking at them. 'This is real?' he says. 'All this you are telling me?'

More real than me or any of those others on the bus getting to run in the junior Olympics; bees to the honeytrap, that's all we were. 'It's real,' I tell him. 'Are you ready?'

'I am ready.'

Thank goodness for that!

I sling my bag off my shoulder and onto the floor, slip out what Blake called 'the Blake design super-light-alloy fold-away-to-almost-nothing wheelchair'.

'What's this?' Ahmet looks bewildered.

It's as complicated as a three-dimensional sudoku puzzle, that's what it is. I click out the parts, jab a loose rod into a likely hole, snap out a pair of arms, and mutter at wheels that look nothing like wheels until they too fold out and click into place. 'Here.' I toss him rolled-up yellow overalls, disposable. 'Put them on and pull the hood over your face as much as you can.' There. Finished. Twenty seconds. Not bad.

In the background I can hear a beeping; it sounds like an alarm to me.

'You're going to wheel me out?'

'That's right.' I tear off my white coat and put on my overalls which have 'SIC' splashed in big red letters across the back and on the front, too. 'Special Injuries Clinic,' I tell him. 'You have to look half dead. Shouldn't be difficult.'

'I am tired, it is true.'

'Are you kidding; they've drained you. Here, get into the chair.' I bundle my discarded white coat and stuff it into the bag. 'Let's go.'

We hit the double doors at a run. They bang wide and we shoot through. One or two of the washed-out runners look at us with some foggy surprise. The table tennis players freeze mid-shot and gawp. And we're past. Bang. Another set of doors.

I've no choice but to go back the way I came in.

'Oi!'

It's the gorilla. No surprise there. Can't let him see my face though, even someone as dim as him is going to register I'm playing Mickey Mouse with the rules. Just let him see my back, that is my stunning master plan.

'S–I–C!' I yell over my shoulder. 'Emergency!'

Beep. Beep. The alarm is still nagging away.

Pause while he tries to register this and I make another ten yards. 'Oi! You didn't pass me on the way in!'

'Twenty minutes ago. Pass number 0042. Other door...' Keep going. Keep going. I hit the lift button as I hear his feet pounding along the corridor after me. If the lift is there, we have a chance. If not...

A voice on the internal tannoy announces my name: 'Michael Patroclus, please return to the visitors' desk in the front hall. Michael Patroclus please return...'

That's exactly what I am doing!

The lift door opens and I slam Ahmet through, jump in after him and punch the close button. 'Sorry,' I call back through the closing door. 'Every second counts.' It certainly does.

There's the guard's face.

And now, gone.

Banging on the door above us and then just the whisper of the descending lift.

Ahmet makes to get out, but I push him back in. 'Your best bet is to stay put,' I tell him. The lift chings and out we steam into the lobby.

Head down, off we go. People milling around, but mostly heading for the exit too. Of course: the big address. Good timing, Patroclus. Well, lucky.

'Excuse me, sir...' A horrible and vaguely familiar oily voice and a hand gripping my shoulder.

I feel myself slipping into the panic pool. 'Yes? We're in a hurry,' I say, trying to keep going, but whoever is gripping my shoulder isn't going anywhere that I want to go to. Result? I twist round and nearly tip Ahmet out.

'If you don't mind, sir.'

It's that voice! The weird man from SIRP at the Nationals, the one with shiny black boot-polish hair. This is his clone. Has to be. Smaller, but with round wire-rim glasses and a row of pens in his shirt top pocket.

'Yes?'

'In a hurry, are we?'

Could a black bear beat a poodle in a straight fight?

'Yes, as I said. Urgent. Special Injuries. Ambulance waiting.'

'Perhaps I can help escort you through the crowd, sir?'

What! Another of my father's random expressions pops into my head: 'Beware Greeks bearing gifts,' he sings when he brings my mother breakfast in bed. But I'm the Greek, so I don't need to worry... 'Thank you.' I swizzle Ahmet round and with this stocky SIRP official as my wingman, we cut through the crowd and out of the fairy-tale entrance hall.

There are hundreds of people milling around a stage out on the green area in front of the building. They're not all SIRP officials so there must be guests and celebrities and whatnots for this big announcement, which I suppose is to do with sponsorship.

Overhead I can hear the *thukka thukka* of an approaching helicopter. Sir Pent descending from the heavens; he'd like that. Better if he popped up from a manhole. Everyone watches the chopper settling, wavering slightly as it comes down to land just behind the stage area.

'This way.' My guide surges ahead, expecting me to follow. I look around. There should be a sign of Blake now, shouldn't there? And where's the man going, because he must have noticed that there's nothing resembling an ambulance out here. 'Come on, sir. If you please.'

'Yes.' I make as if to follow. To Ahmet I mutter, 'Get ready to ditch the wheels and strip off the overalls. We're going to have to lose ourselves in this crowd, if we can.'

The man beckons me to hurry. He keeps to the edge of the crowd, heading to the right of the stage.

'Ladies, gentlemen and young sporting hopefuls, we are very pleased to welcome our illustrious Minister for Sport and founding genius of SIRP, the world leader in all things sporting: Sir Maximus Pent.'

There is clapping and a thimbleful of dutiful hurrahs from all those wearing yellow. To my surprise my beetling black-haired guide isn't one of the ones giving out the shout. I take the opportunity to push us into the crowd, hoping to lose him.

Instantly an elderly lady with a giant VIP badge on her lapel jostles up against me. I'm aware of her stooping back and wiry grey hair scraped into a severe bun – the voice isn't elderly though: 'Come on, Patroclus, hurry up.'

The Geek!

The elderly lady grips my arm. 'If you don't mind,' she says, 'I feel a little dizzy.'

Wake up, Patroclus!

I give myself a shake. 'Of course. Please...' I say loudly. 'A little space, please.' If this is the Geek, then my guide, the oily clone, is Blake!

People move aside to let us through and, trying to make it look as though we're not hurrying, I push a little faster. I see the clone looking back, beckoning again. We scuttle up beside the edge of the stage. How does he do it? There is nothing of Blake in his face. Not a thing!

'OK,' he says calmly. 'Farsi, when I give the word I want you out of the wheels and across to the chopper. Don't stop for anyone. Trokka, you and Minou next. I'll bring up the rear. Right, everyone? OK. Go!'

Ahmet jolts out of the chair, runs flat out to the chopper and dives head first through the open door. I'm next with the Geek a few yards behind me. We bundle in together, a tangle of elbows and knees.

'What the devil do you think you're doing!'

An angry face materialises at the opening behind us. The pilot. Has to be. 'I want you out! Right now!' His expression is suddenly round and startled. He makes a little *oof* sound and then his whole body is catapulted out of sight.

'Sorry, old chap,' says the disguised Blake, and

piles in. 'Buckle up, everybody.' He gives a look of disgust at the metal cosh he's got in his hand, presumably what he's used on the pilot. It's a twin of the electric prod that the security guard up on the first floor had. 'Disgusting things,' Blake says with a grimace and tosses it out through the opening. Then he swings the door over and locks it into place.

'Who's flying us?' I ask.

'My dear Trokka. Who do you think?' Blake scrambles into the pilot's seat.

'You're not serious!'

He frowns, ignoring my squawk. 'Ah yes, I see.' He catches my eye and then bursts out laughing. His hands start to move over the switches and dials. 'Mmm, just as I remember. Oh, what's this...'

The engine kicks in; there's a whooshing as the rotors begin to spin.

Outside, I can see people up on the stage turning to look our way.

'Hmm.' Blake scratches the back of his neck and I notice the join where the skin mask meets his actual skin. Creepy, but brilliant!

Then I see Blake sliding what looks horribly like a 'How To...' manual from his yellow bag and balancing it on his knee. Brilliant? I don't think so.

'Do you know what you're doing?' I shout.

Ahmet looks at the disguised Blake and then at me. 'Is there more problem?'

'Just checking one or two...ah. Slightly different to the model I'm used to.' Is that a lego model? I wonder, but keep my lips buttoned. 'This looks like it,' he says.

More and more people are turning our way, and guards are beginning to run. Pent is at the microphone, waving and pointing wildly in our direction.

'Yes!' Another switch is flicked up. The whoosh turns into the solid roar of the rotors at full spin. 'Here we go!' The last thing I see before closing my eyes is this weird black-haired SIRP clone, who I know is Blake really, hauling back on the joystick, and the back of the stage suddenly dropping away beneath us.

It seems Icarus will fly after all.

Chapter 19

Wednesday. 3.50 pm. And only Blake and Minou look relaxed. The chopper, our chopper, nose tilted forwards so that when I open my eyes I see fields and hedgerows and houses skidding away beneath me, is heading south, so Blake told us. 'Pit stop and then the Channel. Fancy a bit of shopping in Calais, Trokka?' he said, followed by a laugh – not the Percy Blake maniac giggle but his Pimpernel laugh, rich as a triple dip of chips. I can't help smiling even though I still feel sick.

The radio crackles and crackles non-stop. 'Red 348, Red 348. This is Tower Control. You are flying illegally. Your flight has been monitored. Return to Cambridge heliport, pad fourteen, immediately.'

'Tower Control. This is Red 348. We are flying under duress...' Blake swivels and winks at us. He loves using what he thinks are fancy legal terms. 'Do not approach. Repeat, do not approach. Threatened violence on board...' He breaks off and then in a guttural voice barks, 'Shut that off. Now!'

'Red 348. This is Tower Control. Are you...'

Blake grins and flicks the off-switch.

'Everyone belted up? Five minutes to landing. We're refuelling, and this is where Farsi disembarks.'

'But you are going to fetch my sister. I must come with you!'

'No chance. This is what we do; what you do is run. You have less than a day to rest and get yourself in shape before you make your way to Wembley for the race. The deal is: you go for that gold, and we go for Soroya. Mr Blake of Blake's Runners is going to meet you and he'll see you get to the stadium in plenty of time. Trust us. We'll be there before the starting gun goes; and we'll have your sister.'

There he goes again. How can he promise this? I'm already running a check list of the things that can go wrong:

- Soroya has been moved and we can't find her
- We find her but the guards aren't dim and we can't get past them
- We're stopped by British Immigration

- Blake crashes the chopper
- Soroya's guards shoot us
- Armed police shoot us
- Somebody else shoots us

Probability ratings? HIGH and climbing.

I abandon the check list; it's not helping.

'You are Pimpernel?' Ahmet asks Blake quietly.

'I am.'

Ahmet sits very still, thinking. I don't believe he has any idea who this Pimpernel really is but he does know that we've all put our lives on the line for him and his sister, and really he has no choice but to agree. 'Good,' he says. 'I will run when I see Soroya.'

'Deal.'

Ahmet looks at me. 'And Michael Patroclus is one of your gang?'

'You could say that.'

He indicates Minou with her grey hair. 'She is old. And she is in your gang, too?'

'Looks can be deceiving. Hold tight everyone.'

We tilt savagely to the left and sweep down in a tight curve. Below is a long brilliant-white flat-roofed building surrounded by a thick black parking area, and beyond the tarmac are rolling green fields.

I can hear Blake muttering to himself as the nose swings up, and we hover for a moment then wiggle down and land with a bump. A small truck speeds up to us from one end of the building while a man hurries out from the front door. Mr Blake. And somehow not looking quite so elderly as he normally does.

'Five-minute stretch.' Blake unclasps the door and jumps down. Ahmet follows.

'One moment,' he says, putting his hand on Blake's arm. 'The deceiving looks. Perhaps your Pimpernel can look different too?'

'Best not to ask too many questions,' says the Pimpernel. He's being friendly enough, but firm too.

Ahmet bows his head politely. 'Of course.'

Meanwhile one of the men in the truck hooks up to the fuel tank while the other loads three black boxes into the chopper. Blake has words with his father who then leads Ahmet, who insists on shaking hands with all three of us first, back to the building.

Blake glances at his watch. 'Time's up.' He signals to the man refuelling to disconnect. Then we clamber back in. Minou sits up in the co-pilot's seat, scuffles the powder out of her hair, straightens up, puts on her own glasses, and shrugs off the dress with the VIP sticker, revealing her usual outfit of

T-shirt and jeans. She kicks off her sensible shoes and slips on her runners.

I sit behind them.

The Geek takes the controls.

What! You know that feeling when icy water shoots down your back in a cold shower? That's me, right now.

I realise that I am squeezing the armrest so tightly that my knuckles have turned bone-white and I've stopped breathing. Of course I've stopped breathing. Why breathe when you're about to die?

She runs calmly through the procedures for take-off, totally unaware of the panic zone right behind her. Maybe it will be all right, I tell myself. Myself isn't listening. 'Ready,' she says. 'Everyone strapped in?'

I try to say yes but nothing comes out of my mouth.

Blake, of course, is totally relaxed. 'Take her away, Minou,' he says. 'You've got the coordinates on the screen in front of you.' Blake leans back and peels off his face mask, then pulls back his wig. 'That's better,' he says, rubbing his face and neck with a cotton pad and shuffling out his hair. 'Had a horrible feeling it was beginning to slip.'

'I had a horrible feeling you might actually turn

into a SIRP slimer; you were very good at it,' says Minou, not taking her eyes off the instruments.

'Thanks.' He gives me a wink. 'Nice to know your friends appreciate you.'

And I think, it would be nice to know what my friends are up to when I'm not around. My voice suddenly slips back into my mouth.

'What are you doing!'

'What does it look like, Patroclus?'

Well, it looks like flying but I'm not in the mood to flatter her. 'When did you learn to do this?'

'Saturdays. With Blake.'

'Saturdays?'

'When you were at the café, Patroclus. What's the matter with you?'

The matter with me is that I think I'm turning green. I take deep breaths and close my eyes.

After about half an hour the English coast slips beneath us and we begin our Channel crossing. Blake unbuckles and clambers into the back with me. 'Let's check the equipment, Trokka. And then I'll run through the plan.'

At the top of box one are some sandwiches and a flask of coffee, which is a good start. Underneath are foldaway bikes, three of them, almost as compact as his special design wheelchair; dry smoke canisters; and the special running shoes in my size. I hold them up.

'I'm thinking tomorrow, Trokka,' he says, 'for the race, but I'll tell you about that on the way home.'

I'm not saying anything but I'm thinking about tomorrow too because I've kissed away my chance to be in the British junior Olympic team. And if my father ever finds out he'll hit ten on the Richter scale.

Blake unclips the second box. 'Now this will be seriously far out, Trokka,' he says, lifting out metal jacket speakers and a chunky audio deck. 'I'm going to hook the speakers up on the outside of the chopper when we've landed. We'll make a blast when we barrel into Pointperdu, shake the place up. I saw it done in a film once, attack helicopters blaring out music. It was brilliant. You'll see.'

'And this?' It's about the size of an iPod.

'This,' he says, looking at it for a moment before slipping it into his pocket, 'is an attachment for my laptop; it'll be the Pimpernel's last trick.'

'French coast coming up,' says Minou.

A minute later we swoop over Calais.

'Bear right,' shouts Blake. 'See the camp?'

I see villages, and a motorway, a swirl of junctions, the sprawling complex of the Channel Tunnel terminal; and then a smudge a little way off:

warehouse, Portakabins, the freight boxes the Geek described, fences, police vans...

'OK, now keep going.' He's glancing down at a map, then looking up to check his coordinates. 'That's it. There. See that, the mill, put her down behind that.'

The Geek brings us in on a gentle arc and we land soft as a whisper on a flat patch of green. Instantly two men and a woman come running out from the mill carrying what looks like a bundled-up fishing net.

Blake jumps down, greets them and then all of us hurriedly pull the net up and over the chopper. Camouflage: even from twenty yards away it looks surprisingly like a green hillock. The woman slips Blake a folded piece of paper and then the three of them shake hands with each of us, wish us all '*bonne chance*', jump on their mopeds and shoot off.

The Geek and I know better than to ask who they are. Blake, as the Pimpernel, has more contacts round the world than Times Newspapers Inc. He glances at the paper the woman gave him. 'Excellent. Soroya's guard likes to order pizza and chips from Marie's café in Pointperdu village, and we now have his mobile number.'

'Are you planning on asking him to let her go?' says the Geek primly.

'In a manner of speaking, that's exactly what I'm going to do...' He grins and rubs his hands together. 'A little bit more complicated, of course, or it wouldn't be fun. Come on, we'll shift the equipment into the mill and then have our supper while I tell you the plan. No rush. We can't do anything until it's dark.'

It's 6.30 pm. Two hours till sunset. Twenty-one hours to the start of Ahmet's race.

'This is how we do it. You two cycle in, no one's going to stop you. Minou guides you to the freight box where Soroya's locked up. I call the mobile to get the men out of the way. Minou makes contact with Soroya so she knows what's going on and then scrambles up onto the flat roof and marks it with the paint so I know exactly where to bring the chopper. Trokka cracks open the door. Minou said it just had a bar on the outside but in case there's a lock, you better take this. You pull the trigger. Squirts in a liquid that'll instantly freeze up the metal. Then you whack it with this.' He hands me a hammer. 'And Bob's your uncle. The lock shatters and in you go. Bring out Soroya. As soon as I see the sign I'll have the chopper overhead. Brilliant. Just like that famous escape when the chopper came right down in the middle of the prison yard. I won't even land though. Down with the harness and Minou and Soroya can get in together, I reckon. Then we drop it for you, Trokka. The whole thing, two minutes flat. Here, take this, too.' He slips a pen-shaped cylinder into my jeans pocket. 'Flare. In case you get shipwrecked. Just twist the top and chuck it.'

Flare. What do I want a flare for? He's got gadgets on the brain. 'And if the guards come back before we're done?'

'Plan B. You use the three bikes to cycle out of there and I pick you up when you hit the road.'

I glance at Minou. Great. A bicycle getaway. It doesn't appeal too much. Might give us an edge cutting through the camp, but once we hit the outside anyone with a motor is going to run us down before Blake can bring the chopper to us. The French riot police for a start. I say, 'What about the armed police?'

'The boys in blue. No fear, bro', diversionary tactics will be employed.'

'Is that what's in the third box?'

'Absolutamenti.'

'Don't use that word!'

He grins. 'It'll be the perfect tube.'

What's he talking about?

'When you're surfing, Trokka. Come on! It's when

the wave turns into a tunnel and you surf right through it. How cool is *that*! I bet Minou would be up for it, wouldn't you, Minou?'

'I don't like sand,' she says.

He looks hurt. 'Where's the poetry in you two? The sea's our next big thing: Blake's Longboards, Blake's Sharksnapper Boards... What do you think?'

'Stick to runners,' says Minou.

Chapter 20

While Blake fiddles with his speakers, clamping them to the underside of the chopper and then making the wiring secure, the Geek and I take it in turns to keep watch on the camp through a pair of binoculars.

From our position up on the top floor of the empty mill I can see the Red Cross office clearly. There's a long queue of people lining up to go in and a dismal sprinkle of people coming out. All the time I'm watching, I can see a group of men standing around, eyeing the queue, sometimes calling someone out of the line, talking to them. They don't look like officials. No way. I wonder if they have anything to do with the gang holding Soroya.

The main gate is directly opposite the office and although there are a couple of policemen outside it, there do seem to be quite a lot of people going freely in and out, just like Minou described.

We keep watch on the camp until dusk falls and lights begin to speckle the buildings. Then we kit up and unfold the bikes. I'm carrying the spare one in a square case, wrapped in brown paper and tied up with string – it weighs nothing; the Geek has the paint and all the door-busting material. We've changed – nothing clever, just the same kind of worn jeans and T-shirts that the people in the camp wear.

Blake's not happy though. He eyes us critically and says: 'No! That won't do at all! Here, wait a minute.' He runs off and comes back a moment later with a bucket full of muddy sludge which he slops over the bikes, mainly on the wheels and chain. 'Too new. That'll do the job now.'

'Thanks.' Minou looks disgusted. 'Are you sure it's just mud?'

'Pure mud...with a bit of grease and engine oil. You'll be all right. Good luck.'

'Thanks.' Maybe it will be as simple as he says. Maybe.

We do what Minou did the first time round and casually tag onto a small group: a mother with her little daughter and two men, one much older than the other, both carrying straw shopping bags filled with vegetables.

We make a big thing of talking to each other, and Minou speaks the loudest, in French, so it'll seem we're not at all bothered by the two policemen standing in a pool of light by the gate, watching us. Hard men in heavy boots and uniforms with more pockets than a mutant kangaroo, and each pocket, I imagine, stuffed with a weapon. Stun grenades. Tear gas. Cockroach powder. You name it, I bet they've got it. They both have guns of course, automatic rifles of some sort. Their fingers rest lightly on the trigger guard. Behind them are two gleaming motorbikes. They look bored. They look at us like it's our fault they're bored.

'*Eh!*'

I look back and wiggle on my bike, almost tipping into the Geek. The 'eh' is obviously for us. Brake or accelerate?

'*Arrêtez!*'

That sounds a like a serious 'stop!' to me. I brake and put my foot down.

The policeman takes a step towards me, indicating the bike. '*Eh, dis-donc, c'est défendu!*'

'*Pardon, m'sieur.*' The Geek nudges me and dismounts. I do the same and the two of us walk the bikes off to the left of the now closed up Red Cross office.

The policeman gives a sour laugh and turns back to his companion. They're going to be a problem if we end up having to race out this way. They're so bored that even bossing a couple of teenagers around is entertainment for them – how much more pleasure will they get kicking those massive motorbikes into life and riding us down? I cross my fingers and pray that we don't have to do the Plan B thing.

I follow the Geek as the narrow path twists left and then right again. There's the smell of cooking and a hubbub of noise, voices, tinny radios, TVs babbling in French, and when we cut down the side of the warehouse we get a blast of Arab music that twists into the night like a basket of snakes.

We pass families huddled round cooking fires. No one pays us much attention and we keep going, walking briskly until we get to a stretch that seems unnaturally quiet and dark. The Geek signals me to stop. About thirty paces ahead I see the red glow of a cigarette. 'That's one of them,' she whispers.

We pull into a narrow gap between two container boxes and I take out my mobile and text Blake. Once I've received his signal, a single 'P', I know we have less than five minutes before he's overhead.

A moment later we hear a phone ring, one of those loopy ringtones that make you want to batter the stupid thing with a sledgehammer. 'Yeah?' The voice is a growl, suspicious and as English as sausage and mash. There's a moment of silence as the guard listens. I would love to hear what Blake is saying, but whatever it is our 'friend' is nodding. 'Yes. I see, sir. You'll be there. Of course. We'll both come.' He snaps the phone shut and I see the butt of the cigarette arc out into the alley. He turns and bangs on the door. 'Get your ass out of there, Jigger. We've got business in the village.'

A second man comes out and then the metal door clangs shut. A bolt is slammed over and the first man fumbles with a key. We hear a muffled voice complaining from inside. 'Belt up, princess,' he snaps, 'or you'll end up on the inside of a concrete mixer.'

His friend laughs. 'Beat you at chess again, did she?'

They saunter down the alley and we press back into the darkness as they pass us. I catch a whiff of stale tobacco smoke and cologne.

The Geek raises her eyebrows and I nod. It's clear. We slip out of the shadow and run to the freight box. We prop the bikes against the side wall and I put down the third one. I get out my tools as the Geek slides round the end of the box to where she said there was a grille-covered window. I hear her tapping and whispering.

At first there's silence, then an excited cry, cut short, and then a gabble of questions. I hear the word 'Ahmet' several times.

'Shh!'

Then: 'Patroclus! The door.'

I get to work but immediately have to stop to give Minou a leg up so she can reach the roof. I pass up her bag and then start on the lock. I squirt in the liquid. It has a sharp smell that bites the back of my nose. I give the lock one, then a second booming whack with the hammer. It cracks. I pull back the bolt.

I can hear the sound of a chopper in the distance. 'Give it a push!'

The door opens and a tall dark girl stands in the opening, outlined by the yellow light of a gas lamp. She has the face and the same way of standing as Ahmet. Her head is covered in a black shiny scarf and there's the bullet pendant round her neck that Minou had described. She looks at me, her expression tight with worry. 'Who are you?' she asks.

'Patroclus,' I say, 'and you have to get up onto the roof. Do exactly as my friend Minou tells you and we'll be out of here in a couple of minutes.'

'If that man come back, he will kill me,' she says, 'and Ahmet too.'

'No one is coming back,' I say. 'You ready to jump?' I help to hoick her up and Minou catches her hand and gives her a pull. She skiddles up the side and onto the roof easily, much more so than Minou was able. An athlete, I think, like her twin.

We can clearly hear the sound of the helicopter now, the *thukka thukka thukka* of its rotors chopping the night air. It makes me think of my father slicing tomatoes. The sound of some thundering classical music booms down from somewhere above us, then we see the chopper balanced on a pillar of moving light, and the harness swaying under its belly like a snake.

'A breeze!' I call out to the Geek. Only Blake could do this.

'What?' The Geek has her hand to her ear but she can't hear me. He's right overhead, the light picking out Soroya like she's a star on a stage. I shake my head. It doesn't matter. It's crazier and bigger than anything that's happened before. A helicopter rescue ...and in France, too! Not that we'll be able to tell anyone it was us; we'll just read about it in the papers and keep our mouths shut.

Soroya snatches the harness. The Geek is waving at me. I wave back, grinning like a madman.

What an idiot! She's not waving, she's beckoning, frantically. Something's very wrong. She can see something I can't. There's a crackle and a pinging sound. The chopper's light goes out.

A loudspeaker starts up. '*Attention! Attention!*' and something about '*restez dedans*'. I run at the side of the freight box and try to kick jump up it. My hands slap the side, fingertips touch the rim but not enough to grip it.

For a second Minou's face is close to mine. 'Hurry up, Patroclus!' Not the usual calm Minou, I register as I drop down, twisting away from the side as I fall. I land, knees bent, crouching, ready to go again. And now I see what the Geek was getting so stressed about: there's a gang of people running and shouting and pointing. I don't know whether it's at me or the chopper but I don't want to stick around to find out. I back up and take another run, hurling myself up, jabbing with the toe of my runner, trying to get a grip where there is no grip to be got.

I just touch the rim this time. All I need is a tweak, a lift, a hand, but the Geek's not there when I need her and I drop, sliding down the metal, my knees and hands burning and I hit the ground badly.

Someone grabs at me, but I'm like an eel. If I stop, I've had it. I roll and keep rolling, then get up on my feet, ignoring the jab in my ankle, and dive down the narrow gap between this box and the next.

'Arf...!' A grizzled face and a bulging belly ram themselves into the gap after me and stop, an arm flailing at me. He's stuck. But so am I. My escape route narrows to a slice of nothing. 'I'll have your guts, you sneaking little rat. You come back here or I swear I'll stretch your gizzards from here to the Tottenham Court Road.'

Nice offer, I think, as I drop to my knees and peer under the freight box. Minou said she'd crawled under one and anything she can do I reckon I can, too.

It's a squeeze but I sort of fold myself into the space under the box, and then wriggle as fast as I can right down the length of it, heading I hope to where we have dumped the bikes. Out from under one, across another narrow space, under the next. The noise above me is like a muffled storm: the crowd yelling, shots pinging, loudspeakers, an orchestra thundering and the helicopter, still there, hovering above us. My knees and elbows are raw and burning; I'm slick with sweat; and the smell under here is about a hundred times worse than the school toilets.

Somethings scuttles past my face.

Rat.

Yuck.

But rats are smart. They survive. Come on, Patroclus, be cunning, be quick. I poke my nose out of what I reckon must be the last of these freight boxes.

Yes!

There are the bikes. I slither out and come face to face with a boy about my age. Is he going to yell, bring the crowd screaming and yelling for my blood?

He's not even looking at me; I'm probably just another camp scruff to him. A competitor for the prize. He's got his eye on the bikes. No problem. I grab one of Blake's super-neat fold-ups and thrust it at him. 'Take it. Go on.'

'Yours?' he says.

'Yes. Take it.' I shove it at him. He nods and backs out. I grab the other one and peer back at the seething mess of people yelling at the chopper. What they're on about I haven't a clue. The chopper dips and wavers. I can just make out faces at the opening: Minou and Soroya must be safe aboard. Why don't they go? I see a man on the edge of the crowd raise his arm straight, pointing at the chopper. He's careful, taking his time. And then I see the gun, one of those with a clip for the bullets: a machine pistol.

Time for major distraction. Last resort. I take out the flare, pull the popper and chuck it up on to the top of the freight box I've just crawled under.

It explodes in a brilliant blaze of white and blue sparkling light. The helicopter sways, lurches, jigs sideways and then soars straight up into the darkness; the crowd turns like a multi-headed wolf and for a split second is dazzled by the light of the flare. I see the man with the gun nudged off balance. I hear a crack; and then I'm on the bike, standing on the pedals looking for distance, for blue water. Fat chance in this maze.

The crowd yells and surges towards me.

I hit a sharp corner, brake, my back wheel skids round at right angles. I see the boy I gave the bike to up ahead of me, looking back. He jerks his head and sets off again. Lifeline? I make a quick decision: blunder about the camp and end up cornered in a dead end, or take a chance.

I follow the boy, keeping right on his tail. As far as I can tell he's not making for the front gate which is just as well, I don't fancy playing dodgeball with a couple of crophead riot police, no matter how many pockets they've got.

We zigzag, take a blinder right through the main

warehouse, scattering some family's washing, and for about thirty seconds I'm trailing a white cloth from my neck, a cross between a Bedouin warrior and Mr I Surrender. A woman yells at us, and another chucks a bowl of washing-up water at my guide. It hits me smack in the face. I know I need a bath but...well, at least I had my mouth closed. I grip the handlebars tight, and take off through the door, my back wheel clipping the last step and sending me into a freefall wobble. I wrench the handlebars. Somehow keep myself upright and then I'm off again. We've lost the crowd though I can still hear the yelling some way behind us; we've lost the chopper, too; or it's lost us, me. I'll worry about that when I'm out of here.

Our path meets the fence. My guide accelerates down the length of the wire and then brakes, slews round to a stop and points straight at the fence beside him. 'Go!' he shouts.

I don't hesitate but duck my head down and pedal straight for the wire. The bike lifts off as it hits a slight rise and then I'm smacked on both sides by wire as I pass straight through the fence at a point where someone - maybe the boy - has been busy with cutters. I don't turn but just lift my hand in thanks and head straight out into the night.

The ground is rough and hard. I see the road to the right and swerve towards it. Yes! No problem. It'll lead me back up to the mill – that has to be the place Blake will pick me up from.

Moments later I'm up on the road. I stop, just to catch my breath and wipe my face; and then I catch the rumble of a motorbike.

It's one of the cops, not bothering to hurry. Why should he? Not much contest between a 1000-horsepower monster bike and this little-wheeled foldaway. Maybe he's not even interested in me. Maybe he's just heading home for tea. Maybe I'll be lucky.

And maybe not.

I twist the wheel round and start cycling full-tilt away from the camp. If he wants to arrest me then he'll have to come and get me. Stupid. What kind of a lead have I got? Half a minute? Fifteen seconds?

I hear his engine gun from rumble to roar and at the same moment I hear the helicopter whining down, the music suddenly double-loud, a blast of solid old-fashioned pomp-rock. '*And another one bites the...*'

I snatch a quick glance over my shoulder. The chopper's really low, like it's almost hanging on the French cop's shoulder, and the cop's bike is wobbling as if it's getting buffeted by the walloping thump of Blake's crazy music: '*And another one bites...*'

And the next second the cop seems to lose balance and suddenly veer off the road; and instead of running me down he's smoking across a dried-up field. '*Another one bites the dust, and another one...*' The chopper drops down even further, six feet and easing lower, coming in from my right.

I see someone leaning from the opening – it must be Blake, though he's got a Zorro mask on, and his hand is down ready to grip mine. So close now...

I reach up. Our hands slap together and with a yell I let go of the bike, swing my other hand round and grip his arm and we're away, dangling in midair, the wind pummelling me, the motorbike streaking towards us, its headlight bouncing up and down because of the rough ground. My stomach's hanging from my toes, my eyes are streaming, my arms aching. But the Pimpernel's got a grip like iron. I see his mouth going, 'One, two and...' And with a heave I'm up and sprawled on the floor of the chopper. The door is slammed shut and we tilt and sweep up into the night sky. The Geek is at the controls.

'Why do you always have to make things so difficult, Patroclus?' she says.

Chapter 21

It's a joke. I know it is. The Geek makes jokes that always make me think of pancakes, flat and needing a lot of sugar.

'You all right, Michael?' asks Blake. There's concern in his voice. I guess the Zorro mask is for Soroya's benefit. She's sitting strapped in, staring at me, a look of horror on her face. I must look terrible and probably smell worse.

'I'm OK.'

The chopper lurches and Blake grabs a strap to save himself being thrown against the exit door. It steadies and then gives another lurch, dropping suddenly before picking up again. The engine has picked up a new sound, like a cough.

'Fuel,' says the Geek. 'We're low, must be leaking.'

Blake scrambles over into the co-pilot seat. 'Range?'

'Thirty miles, maybe a bit more.'

Blake glances back at me. I shake my head. It's going to be too tight; the tunnel's thirty-one miles long. I looked it up. I almost wish I hadn't. As for getting to Wembley Stadium, that's out of the question.

Soroya, seeing the look on our faces, asks: 'What does this mean?'

'Don't worry,' says Blake, his voice suddenly brisk, 'we'll get you there in time.' To Minou, he says, 'Change of plan,' and reels off a series of coordinates. 'Calais,' he says. 'Landing in five minutes. We'll lighten the helicopter. You and Michael will take the ferry and we'll strip the chopper down to her knucklebones. Chuck everything out. That'll easily give us the extra miles. What do you reckon, Minou?'

Can he be right? I look at the Geek. The one and only walking calculator. Her lips move like she's praying as she does her calculations. Then she gives a cautious nod. 'It's possible,' she says.

'Of course it is.' Blake crawls into the back again and digs out a small sports bag. 'Your kit for tomorrow, Michael, so don't lose it. You'll run or I'll eat my hat.'

I nod even though he's not wearing a hat. I nod even though I don't know what he's talking about.

Run? Not unless he can do the magic wand thing.

He gives me a thick envelope. Passports. Cash for travel expenses. 'Two minutes,' he says, taking the controls from Minou. The streetlights of Calais turn from pinpricks into rivers of light as we swoop low over the sea road.

And in that two minutes he outlines how me and the Geek are going to make it to Wembley in time for Ahmet's race. No mention of how he and Soroya are getting back, though.

We dip and then soar over the ferry terminal, bank sharply and then land on the wide, lonely beach in a spray of salty wet sand.

In a flurry of activity, Blake, Minou and I tumble out and, using a power torch, check for a leak. I don't know what we'll do if we find one: run, probably. Plane fuel is more combustible than dragon breath, everyone knows that.

We scour every inch of the fuselage. There are scars and neat little punctures from the shots fired during the rescue, but, amazingly, there's no sign or smell of fuel seeping out. Pimpernel luck.

Blake bites his lip and scratches his head. 'Maybe we burned up more fuel than I reckoned we would. All that skipping about over the camp probably used up loads.'

'Shouldn't there be a spare tank you can switch to in case of emergency?' I ask. I don't know the first thing about helicopters but it's the sort of thing that always happens in films.

'Genius, Trokka!' And Blake practically somersaults back into the cabin.

The Geek gives me a look, and raises an eyebrow. 'Genius?' she says. 'I don't think so.'

Typical Geek that, but she's right because a couple of moments later Blake pokes his head out. 'No go.' He grins. Why! I think sometimes that the more disastrous things get, the happier he becomes. 'OK. That's it! Let's get to work and chuck everything out.'

All of us, Soroya too, get busy. We rip out everything that's at all loose; then we get to work on the seats, safety equipment and anything that doesn't seem absolutely essential. Finally, apart from the pilot's seat, the cabin is stripped down to bare metal. 'Sorry,' Blake says to Soroya, 'it's a bit hard core, but we should only be thirty minutes.'

That's if he and the Geek are right about the fuel; if they're not, they could be swimming the last part of the crossing.

Soroya's already sitting hunched up on the floor, her knees up to her chin. She shrugs. I guess comfort isn't an issue. 'You wear a mask. Why? Are you criminal?'

Blake vaults up into the cabin and then turns back to me and the Geek. 'What do you say, Trokka? Is the Pimpernel a villain?'

'Evil genius number one.'

'You see,' he says. 'Does the mask bother you that much?'

She nods.

'All right, the mask goes, but you have to make a promise never to describe me to anyone. Ever. Do you understand?'

I don't believe it! He is about to break the rule of all rules.

'Yes.' Her eyes never leave his face. 'I promise.'

In a flourish, he lifts it off and flicks it out of the door. I catch my breath. I can tell Minou's surprised, too; she gives a little cough. 'OK. You two, off you go.' He reaches out and we shake hands. He winks. 'See you at the track. Trokka, remember to register.'

'But there's no chance...'

He holds up his hand. 'Trust me. Register. You will run.'

Then he ducks back inside, slams the door and a moment later the rotors start to spin and we back away, shielding our faces from the blast of air and sand. The chopper lifts, ducks its nose and skims out across the blue-black sea.

'Did you know he was wearing another one of those rubber faces under his Zorro mask?' asks Minou, as we tidy ourselves up, pulling on clean T-shirts and brushing the dirt off our jeans.

'No idea,' I say. 'For a moment I almost thought he trusted her.'

'He's the Pimpernel. No one can ever know,' she says. 'Simple as that.'

'Except you and me.'

'Of course, Patroclus. You do state the obvious sometimes, you know.'

I do.

Leaving a stacked-up pile of all the bits gutted from the helicopter, we tramp up the beach, along a stretch of seafront road and into the ferry depot.

Chapter 22

The air's thick with noise and people, people everywhere, shoulder to shoulder, edging and pushing and queuing and asking questions.

'And you are?'

I'm not sure. Four hours' sleep in the back of the car Blake had waiting for us at Dover, and now here we are in the world's biggest mosh pit: Wembley Stadium. I feel as if I've been through a tumble drier.

'I am,' I say.

Minou snatches the document wallet and pulls out my registration card. Well, not mine really, but the one the Pimpernel has somehow conjured up so that I can run – not that anyone will know who I really am because my card says I'm Kahil Giddash from Afghanistan, team member with Ahmet. 'He needs a minder,' Blake had said. 'Look what they tried to do to you at Tornby. They'll try it here. Bound to. Nature of the beast, Trokka.'

Me, a minder! It's a joke really. I'm a shrimp, a mouse, mostly invisible, except when I run. But he's right, of course, that they'll try to block Ahmet. They'll do anything to give their Stick-boy a clear run. So, I'm not sure how I'll stop them, but I'll give it a go. After all, the best runner should win, shouldn't he? And since that's Ahmet, that's the end of it.

'Kahil Giddash?'

'Sorry?'

The Geek sighs. 'His English is not so good,' she says.

I don't think she needs sleep, nor Blake. The two of them were busy making plans while we drove up, Blake phoning in from I don't know where. Probably two thousand feet up in the air. Me? I couldn't keep my eyes open. He still insisted on talking to me, though I couldn't really understand what he was trying to tell me. 'The runners in your pack, Trokka. What are they called?'

'I don't know.'

'Look at them,' he'd said, really excited, like he had some huge discovery to tell me about.

I dug them out and yes, they were good, the best I'd ever seen: silver air-packed soles, thicker than usual but with no weight to them at all: a new grip to the toe for a smart start; silver lightning flash on the tongue. No doubt about it, they were top of the top of the top of the Blake range. 'Wow.'

'Do you get it now? What they're called?'

'Rip?' That was the name stitched down the back in tiny silver letters.

'Yes. Get it!'

Rip? What was there to get? It was a name. What's in a name? 'No.'

'Trokka! Wake up! Rip, like the current at a surfing beach. The rip pulls you out through the surf to where you can catch the big ones. Do you get it now?'

'Oh.' More surfing. I should have known. I find myself only half listening because I don't understand this stuff. The only surf in our town is the wash powder that comes in packs from the supermarket.

'Do you get it now? They'll be in front of you but I'll manage it so you and Ahmet can get through. Just think of the rip. Your running shoes will help too, so don't worry about it, Trokka, you'll be brilliant!'

'Thanks, Blake.'

'Give me back to Minou.' I handed the phone back and I swear I instantly fell fast asleep.

And now this man here, in his stupid little office-thing, is asking me if I'm someone I've never heard of. Kahil who? But the Geek clearly knows who I'm meant to be.

'Yes. This is Kahil Giddash,' she says.

'Giddash. I see.' The man licks his pencil and ticks a box. 'If you ask me, people should all be able to speak English if they're going to take part in the Olympics. I mean, it's our competition, isn't it?'

If my father heard him say that he'd stuff him in a tomato and drizzle him with olive oil.

'I am Kahil Giddash,' I say, trying to sound dignified. I might as well be him because I don't look like me. Not even my parents will recognise me if our race gets televised.

The Geek did the make-up. My eyes look more slanty. My nose is more hawkish, a bit like Ahmet's. My skin's been darkened a bit and my hair is shaved back to a US marine cut. She wanted to give me sticky-out ears like Blake has when he's being dopey Percy, but I wouldn't let her. She was just getting carried away. 'You're so lucky,' she'd complained. 'I just get to watch.' And this is from someone who piloted a chopper! I said nothing of course. I know better than to contradict her, especially when she's got an electric hair clipper buzzing in her hand.

'Well, Mr Giddash,' says the man, 'you'll be

pleased to know that the other member of your team is already registered. The two of you are running in the five thousand? Can't think why your country should want to put all its eggs in one basket, but there you are, none of my business, I suppose.'

'Exactly,' says Minou, taking the number and wrist tag from the man and pulling me away. 'Wake up, Patroclus. We have exactly four minutes and the place is crawling with people I don't like the look of...'

Me, I'm just terrified about the race. I can do two thousand and just about keep pace with Ahmet, or I did when we were warming up, but five... I wonder if I'll be able to keep up.

'Yabba Jabba, what kind of pathetic little creep have you picked up?' Jaco, in bright yellow, pushes out of the crowd to our right; Stef and the Maggot are beside him as usual. The ugliest triplets in the universe. 'And you're holding his hand, are you? How sweet is that?'

She wasn't; she was gripping my arm. She doesn't let go, either. 'Jaco,' she says. 'How come they let you in here? Big day out from the zoo, is it?'

'Oh, the Jabba talks back. That's a change, boys, isn't it?'

'A real change,' echoes Stef with a twisted sneer.

He's not noted for his brilliant repartee, Stef isn't.

'Running, are you?' Jaco says to me. 'In the five thousand by any chance?' They move closer, Jaco glancing left and right. I know what's in his mind; he's about as subtle as an iceberg. Any chance to take out a competitor running against their boy and he'll grab it.

The Geek gives me a tug just as our race is announced.

'Nobble him, lads,' says Jaco, never once taking his eyes off the Geek, but just then there is a surge as the crowd moves towards the stand and we slip away with it, easy as grease, I think.

I glance back and see Jaco's angry face poking between two women who have what my father calls 'a large bosom'. He sees me and mouths: 'I'll have you.'

He won't.

'This way,' says Minou.

'No.' I know he'll guess we'll cut straight to the start line and in this crowd it would be too easy for him to do something – even a hard kick to the ankle and I won't be any good – so I pull her in the opposite direction. 'Go for the stands. Hurry.'

'You won't make the start!'

'I'll run round the stand and get to the start from

the other side of the stadium.'

'That's miles. You won't make it in time.'

'I'll make it. Go!'

We go and for the first time since I've known her I see the Geek actually run. And I run too, the two of us threading through the crowd, trying not to bash into anyone, racing for the stand.

Chapter 23

We make it to the stand where I leave the Geek and sprint round to the far end of the track, reaching the start just as the official is telling us to take our places. I see Jaco and his pals shoulder to shoulder behind the official, scanning the crowd in the opposite direction to where I am. I allow myself a smile. Good thinking, Patroclus.

I take a deep breath and move up to the space beside Ahmet. Other runners are talking to their team-mates or exchanging words with people beside them. Ahmet is on his own, staring blankly down the track. He looks weighed down, sad, not someone burning to win the race. He glances at me and nods a friendly but professional hello. He doesn't recognise me.

'Hello, Ahmet.'

He frowns, puzzled because I'm wearing his country's colours. He says something in Pashtu, his language. I guess it's along the lines of 'I thought I was the only one running from our country. Who are you?' I shake my head. 'It's me, Patroclus.'

I swear his eyes bulge like golf balls. If this were a cartoon, they'd start spinning. 'Is it you?!' Then, as if he can't help himself, he smiles. 'Michael, you are always so many people, like your Pimpernel. And my sister? You bring Soroya?'

'Yes. Yes, we did.'

He scans the crowd. 'Where is she?'

'With Blake. Trust me. She'll be here.'

'Ah yes. Trust.' His smile fades and he shrugs. Then he looks at me again and shakes his head. 'Why you do this? You have your own race, the one hundred, and you're no Afghani.'

'I'm going to ride shotgun.'

He doesn't understand.

'Look who you're running against,' I say.

I glance at the line to his left; we're on the right, our lanes are on the outside. We'll have to push hard to cut in or we'll be hanging onto the outside of the pack, burning up extra distance after the curve.

He looks over his shoulder, at the SIRP boys on

the inside lane. They have the telltale yellow flash on their backs. 'Ah. Them.'

Yes, 'them'. There are three of them, talking together, bouncing up and down in their sparkling new runners, runners I recognise only too well, though they're a good bit smaller than the one I saw being stolen from Blake's house.

Prototype.

Dynamite.

That's what Blake had said.

Trojan shoe. I turn my head away so they don't see me staring, so they don't see me grinning. Of course, he never told me how they would work, not unless that stuff about rips and rip tides was his way of explaining. I don't care. We're in with a chance so I have just got to do what Blake said – trust him.

Funnily enough, the boys in yellow are doing just the same as me, deliberately not looking our way, or Ahmet's way really since they wouldn't know me from Adam. I know them though: they're the same thug-runners who knocked me out of the race at Tornby and then tried to have me banned for cheating. Nice.

And nice for Sir Pent if his Stick-boy picks up gold.

'Shotgun is like...' Ahmet searches for the word, 'guard?'

'Yes.'

I stretch my hamstrings and try to look tough even though I know that me trying to look tough is a bit of a joke; and not much of a comfort to Ahmet. There's only one thing he wants. 'She's safe, Ahmet. I promise you.'

The truth is I don't know where she is. Somewhere with Blake, and all Blake said to us was that he would 'pitch up' and we wouldn't be able to miss him.

'She will be here,' I say. 'The Pimpernel gave his word.'

'Ah. Famous Pimpernel and his helicopter.' He gives a half laugh. 'I have more adventures in your country than in my own.'

In the background metallic announcements are listing events, advising people to take their seats. Television crews jostle with equipment, lights blaze and the stadium hums with the excited chatter of a few thousand voices. I see Minou taking her front-row seat. We'll almost be in touching distance each time I take the north-side straight.

Over Ahmet's shoulder I notice a stir in the crowd of officials just a few yards away from us. What's going on? I see Jaco, but it's nothing to do with him. At least I don't think it is; he can't touch me now.

'On your marks.'

Ahmet leans towards me. 'Patroclus,' he says. 'This is great kindness what you and Pimpernel do for me, but I know I cannot win today. You tell me that Soroya is safe, that she is here...and I shall try but,' he shrugs, 'this is it. I tell you already that to win one must only think of the race; I cannot do this.'

'But you'll give it a go,' I say automatically because I'm not fully listening. I've spotted a couple of security men – you can see them a mile away with their dark glasses and those things in their ears. Who's the big shot they're minding? Then I glimpse a figure in a blood-red suit, velvet. It can only be him.

'Of course.' Ahmet smiles and puts out his hand for me to shake.

Behind him I can see the figure in red slowly turning my way, and there's his horrible long pale face, and his pale, staring eyes: Sir Pent.

He sees me and he looks and looks, and I feel like all that careful make-up that the Geek used is being peeled back, leaving me bare. I try not to shudder. I try to pretend that I don't notice him looking at me but I see him speaking sharply to the official, and pointing at me.

The official waves to the starter, making the

'no go' signal with his hands as Pent pushes through to the edge of the track – but the starter hasn't seen.

'I know you!' shouts Sir Pent, his face like a boiled plum; his arms stretched out, one pointing and the other frantically beckoning me. 'You've no right to be in this race. I'll see you never...'

I breathe in. I breathe out.

'Ready!'

'No!' roars Sir Pent.

But it's too late.

Chapter 24

Too late for him because the starter's pistol goes off with a crack and we spring away and hurl ourselves round the bend and down the straight, me and Ahmet trying to angle in to the inside lane; everybody jostling for position. SIRP, Pent and the whole lot of them, even Blake and Minou, are forgotten. I'm a machine now. My chest is tight but my feet are air. I'm on Ahmet's right shoulder and we're safe for the moment but I know that the danger is all ahead.

And there they are, up at the front, a tight knot of SIRP runners in their sponsored kit, blocking anyone who might want to challenge their lead.

But we're nowhere near them.

I find myself urging Ahmet on. In fact I know I can push faster, faster than him. What is this?

'Ahmet!' I'm beside him, on the outside. 'Come on!' But he's staring ahead, like some kind of hollow man. Not hearing me. Not hearing anything.

'Ahmet!'

We take the first bend and start down the straight. I see Minou leaning forwards shaking both her fists and shouting. The Geek, shouting! Not that I can hear anything, the whole stadium is a continuous rumbling roar.

The south bend.

There's blood-coloured Pent, and the yellow Bins clustered together.

'Come on, Ahmet! We've got to catch up!'

I can feel my cheeks jigging, my legs hurting, but it's OK, the hurt is OK. I imagine a gear stick and notch it up a grade. I'm a whisper in front of Ahmet.

'Come on, Ahmet!'

But Ahmet doesn't come on.

Lap two. The stadium erupts into a curling peak of cheers. But we're lagging, badly. If something doesn't happen we're going to trail in so far behind everyone we'll be like last year, forgotten.

Lap three.

Minou's yelling her heart out. I can tell just by the glimpse I get as I pound past. And I hear her this time: 'Pa-tro-clus!' Like that. Chopped up. It makes me want to accelerate. I can't though because Ahmet is like an anchor.

Where are the leaders now?

Miles ahead. I can't help feeling we're so far behind them we might as well get out the deckchairs.

My chest hurts, stabbing on the inside, and I can hear my breathing turn raspy.

I grit my teeth. We can do it.

The long curve now. I keep my eyes fixed ahead, on the two white lines of the lane.

And then I'm suddenly aware of another sound behind the sea-roar of the stadium crowd; a regular, wood-chopping *thukka thukka thukka*, and the noise grows louder and louder until it's a tremendous, reverberating hammering. I'm not sure if it's in my head or in the air above me. I have no time to look.

But I look anyway. And what I see is a helicopter, Sir Pent's helicopter, descending like a giant bug.

The shape of the stadium must be acting as a soundbox because the chopper makes an ear-splitting din, blasting air like a hurricane. And I glimpse Pent reeling away, hands clasped to his ears.

And then clouds of dry ice start to stream from the underbelly of the helicopter, forming a fog into which it slowly sinks. The smoke billows out into the crowd and people scatter like wraiths in the icy grey.

Blake loves to make a showy entrance.

And we're round the bend again. Six more laps to go; my breath is fire. I'm roasting from the inside out but we're so far behind we might as well still be in France.

'Ahmet!'

Who's shouting?

'Ahmet!'

And then I see her, a figure dressed in black, shadowing us on the inside of the track. No scarf. Her shiny black hair flowing free, long legs matching us stride for stride, her thin dark face looking our way.

'Ahmet!'

Soroya!

Did he say it or did I dream it?

'Soroya!'

He roars it.

She's a pace ahead of us, pounding the edge of the track, a black streak, a shadow, a twin.

And immediately I feel the change, like a leash tugging at me, and suddenly I'm struggling to keep up with him.

We edge past France.

Germany.

Neither seem to notice us. Both locked into the race.

Spain.

Keep up, Trokka. Keep up. I'm the shadow now, my foot landing exactly where his takes off.

A little faster and I'm aware that Soroya is no longer with us.

And then at last it's only the SIRP trio ahead.

Ahmet lengthens his stride again and it's so hard to match him. Three thousand metres and he can still accelerate like a Grand Prix winner, eating up the metres between us and them.

Maybe they've heard the yelling or someone has signalled them because up till now the SIRP boys have been running one, two, three, nose to tail. Now they pull out into a line, blocking three lanes.

Ahmet doesn't hesitate. He just keeps pulling out to the right; he'll circle them, even if it means running right up into the stands, but the SIRP boys drift out to block him; it's like they've got radar in their backs. Ahmet is forced to drop back, doggedly matching them pace for pace, stride for stride.

We pull round the south bend for the last time. I glimpse Soroya waving and bouncing up and down with excitement, and then she's gone.

We need Blake's rip. We need something to pull

us into the front because right now we are stuck; gridlocked. If you can be running with your lungs on fire and still be stuck, that's what we are, stuck in the back row.

I'm starting to hate the back of their necks: sweaty, the muscles pulsing. And their breathing: all three puffing in unison. I'm behind Stick-boy; Ahmet is on my left.

'Move over!' I say.

Puff.

'Muck off,' he replies.

My eyes fix on Stick-boy's fat-heeled Trojan runners. Shiny-white and peppermint-green, slapping the rust-red track.

Puff.

'Move over!'

Puff.

'Muck off.' Puff. 'You widget.'

Widget? He calls me 'widget'! What's a widget? I don't know what it means, but it makes me mad. I press closer, as close as I can, and I know I shouldn't do this even as I'm doing it but I let the tip of my running shoe catch the fat heel of Stick-boy's, just like they did to me at Tornby. But he doesn't trip, just loses his rhythm for half a second. That might have been enough to let Ahmet through but the SIRP boys keep the line, shoulder to shoulder.

'Get him!' Stick-boy has a thin, raspy voice, scratchy as a match. Instantly the one on the left drops back a pace, deliberately jarring into me, cracking me hard with his elbow, forcing me to pull back.

Ahmet glances back at me, but says nothing.

Where's Blake? Where are all his rip tides and currents that pull you through! Now would be the moment...

This happens to me when I'm running. If I'm not careful my mind begins to wander and I start having conversations in my head and then my running loses its rhythm. In half a second I've dropped a full metre behind Ahmet.

So what? I'm not doing any good anyway. All this: the rescues, the disguises, getting chased halfway round northern France, all this... I've a sour taste in my mouth and and I think of a new rule. Rule thirteen. The unlucky number rule.

Don't give up.

I gulp air like a goldfish and try to pick up my pace.

Round the west curve, coming up to Minou again. There she is, leaning forwards, still shaking her fists and yelling at us.

And Soroya, in the stand beside her now, still waving. There's someone else with them too, a stocky little man next to Minou, head down, bowed over something like a laptop. And Minou's mouth is as wide as the Blackwall tunnel and what she's yelling, I suddenly realise is: 'Now!', and her thumbs are pointed up. It's Blake with that thing he called the Pimpernel's last trick!

Whatever is going to happen, it's in this moment, this second.

'Ahmet!' It comes out as a gasp. I have my eyes fixed on their feet; three pairs of Blake-design Trojan runners. I try again. 'Now!' I shout. 'Go for it!'

And in that instant, as Ahmet leans forwards into the trio in front, his legs beginning to blur as he accelerates, I see the tiniest puff of smoke punching out from the fat heels of each one of those Trojan runners. In that same split second, the SIRP boys suddenly veer half a pace left and right and Ahmet has a clear track ahead of him.

The stocky man. Pimpernel. Dynamite!

That's what Blake said. Of course, it's not dynamite. That would be stupid, the sort of thing a dim Bin like Stef would do. Blake's done something different, a tiny charge maybe, in the heel of those runners, enough to put them all off balance for half a second, making a gap in their yellow wall that Ahmet bursts through.

The Rip!

Lights pop. The crowd roars.

The last straight and Ahmet is a streaking, air-slicing machine; his legs stretching for longer and longer strides, eating up the distance without seeming to make any effort. While we, me and the SIRP boys, trail in his slipstream.

France comes up on the inside, pushes into second, Germany passes us, taking third place. A hundred metres to go.

Spain and the three plodding SIRP boys are still in front of me. And I am NOT going to be beaten by these yellow vests.

I am Patroclus.

I am Greek.

I don't know what I am or what I'm telling myself but this is it now. Head down. Pump arms. Piston legs.

Fly, Icarus!

Chapter 25

Fourth.

That's what I did. Not a place on the grand podium but not bad for me, Kahil Giddash, a.k.a. Michael Patroclus, Mr Nobody from Peasely. Fourth in the race, but one of three in the Pimpernel gang. And that'll do.

Of course I'd had to spin my family a story as to why I hadn't been running with the British team. 'A mix-up,' I said. 'Wrong name on the invitation. A mistake.'

'A mixer-hup. Always a mixer-hup.' My dad gave me a hug and I could see he wanted to ask questions about it, but I just looked at him and shook my head, and he nodded and let it go.

Ahmet Farsi was up there, top of the stand where he belonged, and his country's flag was the one flying above all the others.

'Michael! You should be this one runner.' My father is twisting up a dishcloth as if he's strangling a cobra as we watch the rerun of the race. 'My goodness. He is fast, very fast and this boy, see this boy, he should be Greeks, Michael, this boy.' He's pointing at me on the TV though he doesn't know it.

'His hair is cut like yours, Michael!' That's my mother. Trust her to notice something like that.

'You are a so silly woman!' exclaims my father, shaking the dishcloth at her but not taking his eyes from the TV. 'Why you talk about haircuts. This boy should be winning too. Look! See how he pass those filths in yellow! The world see how they cheat!'

Of course we recorded it and watched it again down in the café: the whole family and Minou and Blake. A real party. And as for me coming fourth, who cares! It gave me such a glow to see Ahmet running his brilliant rip, and yes I got a weird proud feeling watching the way, right in the last stretch, this funny-looking boy that was me seemed to pull a bag of speed out of nowhere; his face grimly determined. Nothing was going to stop him, you could see that, and he seemed to claw his way past the three SIRP runners, one after the other. Each of them turned his head as he passed, looking sick as dogs. But he didn't look at them, and as he ran the last thirty, twenty, ten metres, they fell further and further behind while he just kept getting faster. Flying.

I wanted to cheer myself, to jump up and down and yell my head off!

Don't worry, I didn't. I grinned, my face hot as a boiled kettle, and kept my mouth shut.

Anyway, the Geek would have ticked me off if I'd said anything. She's already told me that running round in circles isn't that special.

Blake was the noisy one, of course, he whooped and yelled every time we saw Ahmet doing his rip-run and every time I pushed past to make it to fourth. 'I said you would run, Trokka,' he muttered in my ear. 'And that was total, a dream pipeline. I knew you would do it. Just knew it.'

He made it happen though. He made the rip. A bit of luck, a bit of cunning. That's what he said. 'Knew how they'd think, Trokka, that's the key. The proto had a tiny bit of wiring in the green thread that ran to a micro-electrical charge in the heel. The SIRP scientists copied it exactly, copied every last bit.' He laughed, delighted with himself. 'So all I had to do was trigger the charge. There's a little dink which they don't even feel, and a tiny bit of rubber goes into meltdown. That's it. They're off balance. Wipe out.'

He gripped my shoulder. 'Next time, we won't have to do any of that stuff. And I swear you're going to run that race again, but as yourself. Then we'll see *you* up on the podium.'

Well, maybe. Don't count chickens, that's my motto. Chicken-counting is stupid. And to tell the truth I don't think I want to be up on that podium and do all the things Ahmet had to do, the interviews, the press and the cameras and all that.

He made a good speech about how the Olympics was to do with nations coming together; about friendship more than competition; and he talked about how his country needed the friendship of nations – not muscle or bullets but friendship and help. Then he talked about us, not by name of course, just that when he needed help he found three friends in this country who helped him win the race: one was English, one was Senegalese and one Greek...

We had said our goodbyes to Soroya and Ahmet after the speech and the main ceremonies were over, and before any journalists started sniffing around to find out if there was a story about these friends of his. There was, of course, but it doesn't belong to them. It's ours.

When we were watching it all again, back in the

café, we didn't get halfway through Ahmet's speech and the thing about the friends who had helped him before my father slapped the table and started to shout. 'Greeks! Of course it must be Greeks, his friend who help him. The Olympic is Greek. Michael,' he points his finger at me, 'remember this, you are Greeks. You should run. You will win this, too.'

'Yes, Dad.'

And then my father started to sing and my mother sang too and they danced. Even my sister danced. And they made me and Blake dance, hands outstretched, stamping our feet, before my mother pulled Minou onto her feet and the Geek danced! She didn't smile though, not even when my mother pinched her cheeks.

'I was concentrating,' she told me later. 'You have to count when you're dancing, didn't you know that? In fact I think it's easier flying a helicopter than trying to dance with your family, Patroclus. I should have known your family would make it complicated.'

Postscript

That wasn't quite the end of it.

I mean, of course we reckoned it was a victory and it was really. Ahmet did win, Soroya was rescued. The three SIRP boys should have been disqualified from running ever again; they tried to pretend their blocking of Ahmet was just accidental and that they hadn't elbowed the other Afghani runner, Kahil Giddash, but everyone knew it was cheating. It was all caught on camera anyway; it made great television. But they weren't disqualified because Ahmet wouldn't testify. Perhaps he felt that the truth would be a bit too complicated. And of course no one was able to find Kahil Giddash. He apparently flew straight back to Kabul after the race. Apparently.

There was quite a scandal about the SIRP sports company – newspapers sniffed about and there were stories of a film supposedly showing SIRP employees breaking into a rival company – that was Blake's footage from the camera hidden in the shoe. But somehow nothing came of it.

Mr Pent even appeared on television. He wriggled and writhed in front of the camera, denied that SIRP was involved in anything as disgusting as cheating or stealing. SIRP was forward thinking. SIRP was about helping young runners to achieve. The SIRP Academy was a beacon for young runners. It was an outrage that some unscrupulous competitors were suggesting that young athletes were being tricked into signing up for a training course and then being used as guinea pigs for research. It was outrageous. SIRP was at the cutting edge of sport; the cutting edge of design.

And then followed a pure Pimpernel moment. The three of us were together, Blake, me and the Geek, watching Pent on the news up in my room, just talking quietly, wondering what else we could have done to get rid of him once and for all – when to prove his point about how cutting edge they were at SIRP, Sir Maximus Pent, in his blood-red suit, produced a brand-new pair of running shoes.

Blake hugged himself. 'It just is not possible,' he said.

'What?'

'Shh. Listen to him.'

We listened.

'These are the ultimate running shoes,' oozed Sir Pent. 'Our design team have surpassed themselves. With these,' he said, holding them up to the camera for a close-up, 'a good runner becomes a great runner, an athlete becomes a champion...'

I looked at Blake. He was actually mouthing the words as Pent was saying them. 'What is this?' I said. 'Did you write his script or something?'

'Yes.'

'With these shoes,' Pent purred, 'a man could run round the entire world.'

Blake clapped his hands together. 'We, my grommies, have ourselves a perfect wave.'

'That is fascinating, Minister. Would you care to trial those shoes for us, perhaps?' said the presenter.

'Yes, of course.'

We watched as Pent eased off his expensive-looking, creepy suede shoes and poked his silk-socked foot into the first runner.

'Are these the second pair that were stolen?'

asked the Geek quietly. 'The ones you designed for Patroclus?'

'The ones you said had a major fault in them?' I added.

Blake smiled.

On went the second runner and Pent stood up. 'There,' he said, and lifted himself onto his toes. Then he gave a couple of little bounces as if he was beginning to limber up for a run. 'They, um, do make you feel like running,' he said. 'Completely marvellous. Cutting edge, absolutely.'

'Well, go ahead, Minister,' said the presenter. 'We'll have the camera follow you.'

Pent smiled his pale smile and took a couple of jogging steps across the studio, and then a couple more, and then circled the studio, and started running faster... Someone opened the door, and he ran out, down the corridor with the camera crew following.

The next shot was of him on the street and the presenter was breathless and shouting: 'Minister, that's fine! Thank you!' But Pent was still running, a blood-red figure bobbing along the street, his spiky knees practically hitting his chin, and all the time weaving clumsily through the shoppers, bumping into people, his head turning this way and that. He looked frantic, panicky, as if he wanted to stop, but his legs wouldn't let him. He collided with a huge bruiser in mirror glasses who kaboomed him with both hands, slap in the chest, and sent him spinning like a top into a poor mum with her two daughters. He flattened the three of them. And that didn't stop him either; his legs did a sort of spindly squiggle in the air and he was over them.

Then the camera crew clearly just gave up, because the last shot was of Pent cantering right down the middle of Oxford Street, taxis and buses screeching and squealing to avoid him. And then he was gone.

It was brilliant.

Wicked.

Blake told us that the shoe he had designed for me had a little electric pressure point that would tap into the nervous system, to give the legs a bit of a boost. 'Thought I could make you a marathon runner, Trokka. Didn't need to though, did I? You went the full distance, no problem.' The real problem was that he couldn't quite get the design right. He wanted the pressure point to cut in when the person running found himself tiring, but he could only get it to come on and stay on. He reckoned Pent probably was running flat out for about six hours, maybe longer. Maybe he ended up in Scotland.

Well, he ran right out of the news and right out of public life, too. And we've heard nothing of him since. Exit Sir Pent.

So, a sort of a victory.

As for us, we exit kind of differently. I told you that the Pimpernel loves showy entrances but he also likes to slide away unnoticed.

And that's the way we do it, the three of us, the Geek, the Greek and the Pimpernel – we fade into the crowd. That's it. Just drift out of sight, like the dry ice at the stadium.

We're still here, of course. The Pimpernel never disappears – it's always around, such an ordinary little flower that nobody really notices it, like the way nobody notices us. And that's the way we want it.

THE END

Don't miss...

THE Geek, THE Greek AND THE Pimpernel

WILL GATTI

Staleways School is being run by bullies and thugs – the teachers turn a blind eye and Sir Pent, the corrupt and villainous head, has his own evil plans.

But now someone is turning the tables on the bad guys...

Michael (the Greek), and Minou (the Geek) decide they must find out what is going on. What is Sir Pent up to and, most intriguing of all, who is the mysterious Pimpernel?

ISBN 978 1 84616 367 8

Now read the original adventures of the Scarlet Pimpernel in the novel by Baroness Orczy…

Paris, 1792. The Terror has begun.

Each day scores of the French nobility feed the guillotine. They are trapped in the capital. There is no escape.

But rumours whisper of a league of young English gentleman of unparalleled daring who are risking their lives to spirit aristocrats across the Channel. They leave no trace behind them except a note from the 'Scarlet Pimpernel'.

The ruthless spy master Chauvelin is determined to stop the rescuers by fair means or foul, and, desperately outnumbered, the Scarlet Pimpernel and his men must use all their wits to evade capture and stay alive.

The Scarlet Pimpernel
ISBN 0 340 70762 3

www.hodder.co.uk